W9-CSI-165

THE
DOCTOR'S
WIFE

THE DOCTOR'S WIFE

SAWAKO ARIYOSHI

TRANSLATED BY

Wakako Hironaka and Ann Siller Kostant

KODANSHA INTERNATIONAL
Tokyo • New York • London

Distributed in the United States by Kodansha America, Inc., 575 Lexington Avenue, New York, N.Y. 10022, and in the United Kingdom and continental Europe by Kodansha Europe Ltd., Tavern Quay, Rope Street, London SE16 7TX.

Published by Kodansha International Ltd., 17–14, Otowa 1-chome, Bunkyo-ku, Tokyo 112–8652, and by Kodansha America, Inc.

First edition, 1978
First paperback edition, 1981
First trade paperback edition, 2003
ISBN 4–7700–2974–8
03 04 05 06 07 08 09 10   10 9 8 7 6 5 4 3 2 1

www.thejapanpage.com

INTRODUCTION

The Doctor's Wife appeared in one installment of a Japanese magazine and was an immediate success. Its popularity became so widespread that it was soon adapted for stage and screen.

The story is based on the life of Hanaoka Seishu, who lived in Kishu province (modern Wakayama prefecture) from 1760–1835. From his own personal records, diaries, books, and biography that were placed in a special museum, the author, herself a native of the same area, interlaced authentic and fictitious elements to create a fascinating tale that depicts the rise of a family of peasant origins to a position of wealth and fame.

In the medical practices of that period major surgery was non-existent. Illnesses, grave or minor, were treated by administering herbal concoctions, ointments, moxibustion, and alcohol. It was only with the invention of Seishu's *tsusensan*, an anesthetic, that surgery became feasible. All sorts of operations became possible, including, most amazingly, that for breast cancer. Seishu's first operation occurred in 1805. Nothing, however, was known of this doctor's achievement in the West. In England and the United States the general anesthetics of ether and chloroform were not used until the 1840s.

If medical matters seem to be unduly stressed in the story, it is because Seishu's dreams, ambitions, experiments, and desire for success are the underlying catalysts that propel the two women in his life—his mother Otsugi and his wife Kae—into constant conflict. At first, the relationship between Otsugi and Kae is like mother and daughter, but a change comes abruptly the moment Seishu returns from Kyoto. Henceforth, the women compete for his affection in an atmosphere of perpetual tension. Despite the fact that Seishu is rarely present, his forceful personality dominates the actions and emotions of the women.

The fifteen chapters of the novel constitute fifteen dramatic scenes spread out over some seventy years. Using dialogue rather than psychological analysis, the author elicits the motivations, thoughts, and interactions of the characters. There is hardly a superfluous word, and the few descriptive details are carefully chosen.

Seishu's sister, Koriku, witnesses the female feud from its inception. She alone recognizes that it is her brother's selfishness and total self-absorption that leads to the competition for his affections. Her penetrating, pessimistic judgments in chapter 14 may be considered the crystallization of the author's intentions regarding male-female relations.

> "Don't you think men are incredible?" Koriku asks Kae. "It seems . . . that an intelligent person like my brother . . . would have noticed the friction between you and Mother. . . . But throughout he shrewdly pretended he

didn't see anything . . . which resulted in both you and
Mother drinking the medicine. . . . Well, isn't it so? . . .
I think this sort of tension among females . . . is . . . to
the advantage . . . of . . . every male. And I doubt that
any man would volunteer to mediate in their struggles.
. . . He would probably be considered weak if he did,
and I suspect . . . he would perish like an over-fertilized
mandarin tree."

And in the end she asks the rhetorical question: "Isn't the
relationship between man and woman disgusting?" Koriku,
like her sister Okatsu, sacrifices her life for her brother's career.
Besides, she is used by both her mother and brother as a maid.
At that time many women married if only to avoid this lower
servant status. Koriku's survival was justified by the enormous
contributions she made to the family: weaving in her youth to
support her brother in his studies, and later running the house.
Yet, she regards herself as fortunate because by comparison
to Kae, she lived in relative freedom. Kae's life is always
controlled by someone—father, mother-in-law, or husband.
The point the author makes is that women did not have an
individual existence outside the strict family system. Marriage
meant marriage into the husband's family rather than simply
to the husband. And it is still the case to a certain extent in
Japan today.

A new bride (as Kae's mother points out) had to submit to a
series of tests, failure in which could result in her dismissal and
disgrace. She had to serve her in-laws with obedience and reverence, in almost abject submissiveness. To gain acceptance, she
needed good health and the ability to contribute to the family's
situation and produce a male heir. The new bride secured her
position only after the male heir arrived. Even then she did not

control "purse and kitchen" until her mother-in-law died. In *The Doctor's Wife*, Kae gains control as a consequence of a supreme sacrifice.

Kae was probably more fortunate than many other girls from poorer families. She enjoyed many privileges in the Hanaoka household right from the beginning, besides which, the prestige of her family surely inhibited Otsugi from thoroughly maltreating her.

The marriage between Kae and Seishu takes place in the groom's absence after Otsugi cleverly persuades Kae's father to give his daughter to the Hanaokas. The long, convoluted interchange in chapter 3 must be viewed in light of the fact that while doctors were educated, they were not landowners, and hence were not considered good matches for the daughters of prosperous, influential families.

A final word about Otsugi. The beautiful, clever, assertive woman is responsible for the prosperity of her family. Through her initiative her son studied medicine in Kyoto, and through her arrangement he obtains a suitable wife. In many ways Otsugi is considered the ideal model of a Japanese woman in the traditional setting during the feudal period. The overindulgent, dependent, distorted relationship that often resulted between a mother and her eldest son and the subsequent feuds between a mother and her daughter-in-law are only some of the many byproducts of the family system in Japan.

WAKAKO HIRONAKA
ANN SILLER KOSTANT

The Doctor's Wife

Note: names within the novel follow the Japanese system—family name first, followed by the given name.

I

Kae was eight years old when she first heard of Otsugi and pleaded with Tami, her nurse, to take her to see this woman. One hot summer day the two came to the neighboring village of Hirayama and stopped near the front yard of a ramshackle house. Visible amidst a dense growth of green weeds were refreshing splashes of wild eggplant blossoms, their white petals bearing a remarkable resemblance to the delicate figure which soon emerged.

"Look, child. There she is!"

Awed by Otsugi's beauty, the little girl did not reply.

The story told to Kae described the circumstances under which Otsugi, a daughter of the Matsumotos, had crossed the river to marry into the Hanaoka family in the village of Hirayama, in the county of Nate. Here in the warm climate of Kishu province rich fields flourished along both banks of the Kinokawa River. Now, during the peaceful Tokugawa period,

3

rarely did anything of consequence occur in this remote section of Kishu. But if something did happen, it was sure to become an unforgettable topic of conversation, recounted from one generation to the next.

Only ten years had elapsed since Otsugi arrived in Hirayama in the late 1750s, and all of the people in this tale were still very much alive and talked about. In fact, there was hardly anyone in the area who did not know the smallest detail concerning their lives.

Matsumoto Shinjiro was a prominent landowner who operated a prosperous dye works. As a young girl his daughter was reputed to be intelligent and beautiful, until she became afflicted with what seemed to be an incurable skin disorder. The Matsumotos spared no expense and consulted the best doctors. To no avail. All gave up. But when Hanaoka Naomichi learned of Otsugi's misfortune, he crossed the river, knocked at the Matsumotos' door and brashly declared that he would cure their daughter—providing he could have her in marriage. Desperate, the Matsumotos accepted the condition of the unknown country doctor without hesitation. This was how Otsugi happened to marry into a poor doctor's family.

Naomichi might have earned a brilliant reputation after his spectacular cure. Yet this was not the case, partly because he was too talkative and hence unpopular among the villagers, and partly because his wife overshadowed him with a brightness and beauty really beyond description. Whoever discussed the couple always concluded, "You must see Otsugi. She's incredibly beautiful." The listener whose curiosity was aroused to go to Hirayama was generally surprised to find that Otsugi's beauty truly surpassed the imagination—as it had Kae's.

At that time, Otsugi was about thirty and considered past

4

her prime. But to the eight-year-old, she did not look her age. Despite the terrible heat, she was immaculately dressed in a narrow-striped kimono and tightly fitted sash. Equally impressive were her skin, a milky white like the eggplant flower, and her lustrous hair, impeccably arranged in a high coiffure. The impressionable child never forgot the striking apparition, the freshly shaven eyebrows like those of a bride and the jet-black hair accentuating Otsugi's very fair complexion.

That same day, Kae, bursting with an enthusiasm she could scarcely control, related the incident to her mother, concealing nothing since she did not think it was wrong to have visited Hirayama. Her mother nodded in an approving manner and offered an additional comment of her own.

"Not only is Otsugi beautiful, but she is also clever and wise. I don't know her well enough to judge her intelligence for myself, but those who do speak highly of her."

After that momentous day, Kae began to adore, even worship, the woman whom everyone believed perfect. Had she been older, she might have felt either. jealous or competitive, since she herself was rather ordinary. But at the tender age of eight, no such sentiments spoiled the child's natural admiration of beauty.

Although Hirayama was not far from her village, Kae, the daughter of Imose Sajihei of Ichibamura, seldom came in contact with Otsugi. The distinguished Imose family was in charge of the local village headmen and samurai and, more importantly, entertained the feudal lord of Kishu province whenever he passed through Nate on a pilgrimage to Ise Shrine. As a consequence of their elevated position, Kae was not brought up to run in the fields like the peasant girls of her village. Yet, the Imoses were simple folk. Kae's mother, who was particularly practical, decided from her own experiences with her husband's family to teach her daughter such useful things as cooking and sewing, rather than the refined accomplishments that many girls of her class learned. In addition to her household duties, Kae learned etiquette, reading and writing, and the Japanese customs that were part of her family heritage. At the age of fourteen she was able to cook several special foods which she herself often served to the Kishu lord on the black-lacquered table emblazoned with the family crest. Her parents were proud of her.

While the status of the Imoses did not permit Kae to see the Hanaokas in public places, she found a pretext to enter her grandfather's room whenever Hanaoka Naomichi came to attend him. She herself was quite robust and rarely even caught a cold, so that unless someone in her family got sick, she was not likely to get so much as a glimpse of a doctor.

Long retired as head of the family, her grandfather had transferred his responsibilities to his son, Sajihei. Now, old and infirm, he required medical care more frequently. There were some good doctors in Ichibamura who could have treated him. Moreover, Naomichi was really a surgeon. Yet it was he whom Grandfather chose. It was apparent that Grandfather had a lot of leisure time and found his stories entertaining. The other Imoses called in local physicians.

Since Kae had never taken an interest in doctors before Tami told her of Otsugi, she did not realize how often Naomichi used to come to her house. But after seeing the beautiful woman, she grew impatient to meet the husband. It seemed that she could hardly wait for her grandfather to get sick and send for his doctor again.

The entire summer passed. Whenever Kae entered Grandfather's rooms, he appeared healthy. Sometimes she watched the almost toothless old man noisily chewing on some carp

6

which he especially enjoyed raw. How disappointed she was that he showed no signs of illness!

It was finally winter. On cold mornings Grandfather pretended to be sick so that he wouldn't have to get up. The lack of activity eventually weakened him and he came down with a virus. Naomichi then came to the house with his bag of medicines.

When he stalked through the door, the child who had been anxiously awaiting his arrival, was chagrined. "Can he really be Otsugi's husband?" she wondered, for compared to his wife, Naomichi was ugly. Remembering Otsugi's neat, round coiffure, she gazed in disgust at this unkempt man with his awful complexion, red from too much saké, his thick lips, and his crooked teeth. It appeared that he never combed his hair and that he had slept in his black formal coat, so ragged and dirty it was.

The vision of this unrefined, unseemly person married to the beautiful woman horrified and perplexed the young girl. Over and over she thought of lovely Otsugi in her immaculate striped kimono and wondered how she could ever have married such a man. It was simply impossible for her to imagine them together.

Naomichi's booming voice could be heard in the adjacent rooms as soon as he started examining the patient. His subject matter tended to focus on world events rather than on local gossip, and the old man relished this sort of chatter. Grandfather himself could go on till midnight talking about such grandiose topics as the Tokugawa Shogunate. But his stories were well known, while Naomichi's raised new, interesting issues. Moreover, though an event might have occurred four or five years ago, the doctor had the gift of describing it as if it had happened yesterday. Of course, news at that time traveled slowly to Kishu, so remote from the bustling city of Edo. In any case, the old man listened appreciatively, and was wise enough to discount the less credible portions of Naomichi's tales.

Naomichi was saying: "I assure you, Western medicine will be coming to our country very soon. It was predicted by my teacher, Iwanaga Bangen, when I was his student in Osaka. I think he was right. Because I learned Western methods with him, I can talk with confidence about Japan's medical future, as if I were taking its pulse. In Edo, Dr. Yamawaki Toyo initiated the idea of dissecting the bodies of dead prisoners; the present teacher, Sugita Genpaku, has been pursuing certain Dutch methods which depend on a complete examination of a person's body before a diagnosis is pronounced; this is diffierent from the Chinese approach which relies heavily on the pulse. Ah! The human body is a creative masterpiece. Just look at our fingertips. What a composition of delicate nerve tissue and fluids! . . ."

"Uh, huh." Grandfather seemed fascinated.

"But, as I was saying, now that our central government has recognized the importance of Western practices, it is taking measures to help our doctors incorporate them here. By the way, do you know how many years have passed since those famous doctors Hall and Van Tanno came to our country from Holland?"

Naomichi rambled on and on, no longer even bothering with Grandfather's pulse. "Dr. Hall arrived in 1761, the same day and year my son Umpei was born. When I realized the coincidence, I became convinced that it was significant. I remember that day well. It was the twenty-third of October, at the peak of autumn. The bright, clear sky was suddenly filled with menacing clouds. Then thunder raged and blinding flashes of lightning zigzagged across the sky. At that moment Umpei was born. I myself delivered the child! When the tumult subsided, the birds soared once again in a freshly brightened sky. I cried aloud, 'A genius has been born!' Dr. Hall must have been astounded by his incredible encounter with the weather. Why, no sooner had he set foot on our soil than this terrible thunder greeted him. So, you see, there's no question about the importance of that day. To commemorate the extraordinary event, I called my son 'Shin,' which means 'thunder.' Umpei is his nickname, meaning 'the peaceful cloud.' Great names, don't you agree? I believe my son is destined to broaden the horizons of medical knowledge." The sociable doctor usually concluded by boasting about his son.

Kae pondered the inconsistencies that seemed to surround the doctor. For one, she could not associate the energetic, ill-mannered man with the son he so often described. Then there was the matter of his wife. To be sure, Naomichi and Otsugi were fourteen years apart. But the woman seemed younger than her actual age while the doctor appeared older than he was, which created another disparity between them. No matter how she tried, Kae simply could not accept him as Otsugi's husband.

On Naomichi's visits to Grandfather, he spoke about all kinds of subjects which somehow always ended with his bragging about his son. He vaunted Umpei's most trivial accomplishments, reflecting only the grand expectations he had of him. Because of this, Kae never took an interest in the son. Yet, in spite of Naomichi's numerous negative attributes, she always visited her grandfather when he came.

It should be mentioned that the doctor rarely spoke of his wife. Maybe he knew that Otsugi's past was known to his patient. More than likely though, he was merely following the custom whereby men did not discuss their wives in public; he probably did not wish to be an exception to this rule. Kae tried time and time again to be more sympathetic toward him, but all her attempts failed since she was inevitably disappointed with his appearance and behavior.

II

In his declining years, Grandfather spent many delightful hours with the doctor. Although his health had been fairly good, one day, when Kae was eighteen, without any warning or pain he had a stroke and died gracefully in bed. The Imoses had called their family doctor rather than Naomichi, but by the time he arrived, Grandfather had passed away. It had been more than ten years since Sajihei had taken over the family's affairs, so his sudden death did not cause the Imoses any inconvenience. And among the villagers·the serene manner of his passing was much talked about.

As Grandfather was formerly a powerful headman, there was an elaborate funeral for him. The procedure commenced right after his death, with everyone in the vicinity of Nate coming to pay their respects. Outside the Imose house, a long line formed to burn incense for the deceased. Members of the family were expected to receive these mourners and had no time to indulge their own sorrow. In fact, with so many of their close friends and relatives crowded into the house, the atmosphere was hardly gloomy. At eighteen Kae, of course, grasped the significance of the occasion. But, perhaps because her grandfather's death had been swift and without suffering, Kae, like the rest of her family, was too preoccupied with immediate events. It would be some time before she grieved for him.

For her appearance in public, Kae's parents took special care to have her hair properly groomed and to furnish her with an appropriate black silk kimono. Afterwards, Kae was expected to follow her mother and greet the family guests and villagers. It was then that she saw Otsugi a second time. Naomichi had come to the wake the day before, and had remained in the Imose house drinking through the night. Otsugi, holding red prayer beads and dressed in a hand-woven silk kimono suitable for the occasion, was among the mourners. To Kae she seemed divine, like the Kannon Bosatsu with an azure halo over her head. Kae's gaze was fixed on her alone and could not be diverted.

Others also stared, since Otsugi seldom came to public gatherings. Her presence that day reminded them of her past, and her youthfulness after bearing seven children amazed them anew. Women over forty were generally haggard and unattractive from childbearing and years of hard labor. But Otsugi looked at least ten years younger than her age and quite elegant and dignified in her funeral attire. Kae may not have been the only one to see a halo.

Was Otsugi aware of all the eyes fastened upon her? No doubt, the admiration and attention of others contributed to her youth and beauty. Although her head was bowed in an expression of humility, her back remained erect, and she seemed fully aware of everyone around her. The innocent Kae, however, was unable to detect any hypocrisy. She stood in a trance, gazing at the woman who seemed even more beautiful that day than in the vision she had cherished from her youth.

Ordinary villagers were not allowed to enter the house. They prayed in front of an altar in one corner of the garden, away from the coffin, which was indoors. As a favored friend of the deceased, Naomichi had been shown inside without his wife, which was quite proper on this occasion. Besides, even if it had been fitting to ask Otsugi in, Kae surely could not have done so. She was standing in the garden as if hypnotized when Otsugi filed past her.

Otsugi's kimono was probably part of her dowry and therefore was far better than the costumes of the tenant farmers and other villagers. Made of rough hand-woven silk, it suited her position. However, in view of the fact that the Hanaokas were socially inferior to the Matsumotos, Otsugi's parents had not provided her with a formal kimono of soft shiny silk, wisely deciding she would not have a chance to wear it. Nevertheless, it was a vibrant, rich black, with an elegant degree of looseness at the back of the neck, a neat V-shape opening in the front, and a tightly fitted sash. Otsugi approached the altar and bowed low, revealing a pale green ribbon around the bun of her hair. Kae watched her pick up some incense. As her slender fingers gently rubbed the beads, the young girl could not help thinking that beautiful people were just born beautiful—from head to toe. She also thought that Otsugi's dignity was a manifestation of her superior intelligence. Otsugi bowed toward the coffin in the main house in homage to Grandfather and silently nodded to each Imose close by. Kae had been standing somewhat apart from her relatives and did not expect to be noticed. But when Otsugi, her face shadowed in sympathy, turned in her direction, Kae felt as if the tip of a sword had been pointed at her forehead. The woman bowed to her, not suspecting her feelings, and moved to the gate. As she disappeared from sight, the center seam of her kimono below the sash was still absolutely straight.

III

Three years after the funeral, during the late spring, Otsugi reappeared at the Imoses. Sajihei ushered her into his office, which was set apart from the rest of the house so that he could have privacy in conducting community affairs. But because the area was off limits to women and children, Kae could not discover the purpose of Otsugi's visit from any of the female servants. She wished Tami were at home to advise her, but the nurse had gone to purchase some yarn for Kae and had not returned. Curious, yet not overly inquisitive, Kae eagerly continued her embroidery, never dreaming that the conversation between Otsugi and her father concerned herself. She made a mental note, however, to find out somehow from her father about the meeting later.

Imose Sajihei could not imagine why Otsugi had come. He invited her in since he wasn't busy, and without delay started the conversation in a cordial tone. Even after three years, the memory of his father aroused a certain nostalgia in him so that he tended to behave kindly toward anyone who had been close to the old man—although he himself had little use for Dr. Hanaoka Naomichi.

"How is Dr. Hanaoka?" he inquired politely.

"My husband misses your father very much and seems to have aged since he died. I am here today on his behalf."

"That's nice of you. Now tell me, what can I do for you?"

"I have come to ask for your daughter Kae's hand in marriage to my son Shin."

Sajihei was stunned. Surely she was joking. The present Imoses, who received a large annual income in excess of one hundred twenty *koku* as law enforcers, tax collectors, and judges, could trace their lineage to the famous clan with a castle at Tanishiro in Nyudani— a lovely castle situated in a valley— and even further back to the Imbe clan. From Gojo to the mouth of the Kinokawa River, the Imose compound, which included quarters for the feudal lord of the region when he traveled, stood out conspicuously on a large tract of land. How utterly absurd for this woman to suggest that he, Imose Sajihei, from a distinguished family, agree to a marital arrangement with the family of an impoverished doctor! Displaying an embarrassed grin that was meant to convey the impossibility of such a match, Sajihei replied, "Your request is quite unexpected."

But Otsugi, who was perfectly composed and in control, proceeded to explain in crisp, concise language why the Hanaokas desired Kae. And Sajihei, in spite of himself, could not resist listening to her describe the qualifications for a doctor's wife.

"The first requirement is good health. Other essentials are courage, a strong will, and an understanding of the nature of the medical profession, although the woman may not know how to take a pulse. You're aware that a doctor has to be available day and night. Illness, after all, doesn't choose its visiting hours. If he should happen to be out on call, it's up to his wife to manage in the interim. For example, if a gravely sick or injured person arrives she must be able to handle the emergency. A confident, capable woman does not become alarmed at the sight of blood or serious infirmities. Instead, she cleans the wound and so on. . . ." Otsugi barely paused for breath.

"Now, take the daughter of a farmer. Can a girl who spends so much time at the monotonous tasks of hoeing and planting cope with the duties of a physician's wife? I admit that it's sometimes possible for a woman to adapt to a new environment after marriage. But it seems to me that if she has had no education whatsoever, this would be a hopeless expectation. Nor would a merchant's daughter make a suitable wife. No member of a doctor's family ought to be motivated by the idea of profit. What would happen to those patients who couldn't pay their bills? Disease, you know, strikes the poor as well as the rich. I'm sure you'll agree that if the woman of the house is overly concerned with money, she will surely cast an evil shadow on her divinely inspired husband."

The impact of the long tirade was obvious. Sajihei seemed transfixed.

"As for the daughter of a manufacturer, look at her training. I believe she's accustomed to seeing people manipulated, so it would be natural for her to treat the doctor's students and assistants as mere objects. Or she's likely to try flattery to get business. . . . Well, the evidence is clear. The daughter of a farmer, merchant, or manufacturer cannot qualify as a doctor's wife."

The outrageous, arrogant speech would have angered even a

17

gentle person. To be sure, had Naomichi come with such ideas, he would have been silenced quickly and sent on his way. But Otsugi's candor held Sajihei spellbound. And as if she read his thoughts, she hastily added:

"I've told you all these things because I realize that I'm not really suited to my role. You see, I was raised among farmers, merchants, and artisans. My husband learned the best of Western methods, and yet he hasn't amounted to much. I'm afraid this is because I wasn't a good wife for him. To this very day I have tried. But sheer determination isn't always everything. Last spring Umpei left for Kyoto to get medical training. In three years he'll come home. I feel that as his mother I should find the proper wife for him, someone who will encourage him to develop and blossom into a fine doctor. I owe this much to the Hanaokas since I didn't live up to their expectations."

Again she did not wait for Sajihei's response. "Naturally, it's impossible to compare the honored Imoses with my own family, so I'm aware that you might consider my proposal ridiculous and think I lack manners. But I urge you to ask Kae which *she* really prefers—the secure, peaceful life in an already established family, or one fashioned out of her dreams. Maybe she would welcome the chance to build a castle from a shack. I know that she has had a traditional upbringing and that her health is excellent. From every aspect I am positive that she alone would make a good wife for my son."

The easy-going, tolerant Sajihei was not the kind to show anger before a woman or a child. He therefore put up with the aggressive woman until she finished, less out of a sense of obligation to the Hanaokas than as an act of generosity on the part of a village headman. At last he had an opportunity to speak.

"I must give the matter some thought. After all, you've taken me completely by surprise." He accompanied her to the door with a smile, although he had not the slightest intention of considering Otsugi's proposition. In fact, he decided to refuse the offer right away by sending the Hanaokas a message through one of his subordinates.

At dinner that night when he casually mentioned Otsugi's visit to his wife, Sajihei used the familiar analogy of a brass temple bell and a paper lantern to emphasize the impropriety of the match. He raised the subject only to make interesting table conversation, nothing more, since he never planned to consult her in a serious way about the proposal. Somewhat jokingly he said that Hanaoka Naomichi had infected his wife with his effusive, windy chattering, and now the one infected had become more diseased than the donor. Otsugi had probably become slightly deranged, he decided, from brooding so long over her son's future marriage. His wife listened without comment. Sajihei considered the matter finished.

That same night, Kae also learned of Otsugi's wishes. It happened that the maid serving dinner told Tami, who in turn informed Kae. The young girl was overcome with joy, as she had never experienced anything so exciting. She immediately began to wonder when Otsugi had first thought of her and how she had gained her approval. Then Tami reported that Sajihei was not interested in the Hanaokas. The color disappeared from Kae's cheeks, and for the rest of the night she couldn't sleep.

Even more confused was Sajihei when his wife reopened the discussion the following morning. She began by agreeing that Naomichi could barely sustain a large family in his small cottage, and that the Hanaokas were indeed poor, since, she noted, Naomichi had only one student working for him and one young maid to help with the chores. But then she pointed out that despite the fact that the Hanaokas had moved several

19

generations ago into Kishu province, they had not been accepted there until Naomichi married Otsugi. It was afterwards that they expanded their social contacts, probably with the aid of the Matsumotos. Why, Naomichi himself had only been permitted into the Imose home after his marriage.

The conversation grew more heated. "People often talk about Otsugi's cleverness," she continued. "Isn't it reasonable to assume that the Hanaokas' recent successes are due to her? Besides (each word was carefully chosen), no other proposal has been as concrete as this one. Well . . . aren't I right? Maybe Otsugi behaved presumptuously, but the fact is that our daughter would find great satisfaction as a woman in being genuinely desired by the Hanaokas."

His wife's unforeseen concern forced Sajihei to reconsider. As he contemplated the situation, several thoughts occurred to him. First of all, he admitted to himself that it wasn't easy for him to marry off his only daughter. It was true, moreover, that Kae had already passed her prime and that he had declined other propositions, though none had been very satisfactory. More difficult for him to face was the question of Kae's peculiar position as the daughter of the hosts to the Kishu lord, and he wondered if it might have compromised her prospects. Perhaps this had been a strong factor in his wife's decision to look at the Hanaokas seriously. Until very recently Sajihei had been unwilling to consider the subtle implications of what "the daughter of the hosts" conveyed to members of the community. Of course, people knew that Kae was from an honorable family who gave hospitality to the feudal lord. But there was always the lingering uncertainty as to whether she had also spent the night with him. Not that such favors would have been judged dishonorable during the Tokugawa period. Certainly, if the most prominent and powerful figure in Kishu province, who was a relative, moreover, of the Tokugawa Shogun, ruler of all Japan, happened to fancy the daughter of his hosts at dinner, it would have been an honor to serve him afterwards as well. Suppose, however, that he had not requested Kae to entertain him. Wouldn't it have been because she was too plain? And in that case, how could she be proud of her virginity? Sajihei realized that in spite of his enormous influence, he had not been able to prevent all kinds of rumors from ensnaring his daughter. And if the lord wanted to "honor" her, she would be a light evening's sport anyway, not even his mistress afterwards. Meanwhile, she was still living with her parents at the age of twenty-one with no other prospective marriage.

Arms folded and deep in thought, Imose Sajihei evidently could not find a solution. Not that he shared any of Otsugi's views, but he did grant the special status of the doctor in as much as he did not belong to any of the four social classes, namely, samurai, farmers, artisans, and merchants. And it could be argued that men of medicine should not be denigrated since they were well educated and served society in a benevolent way. Moreover, most doctors were known to be the second and third sons of wealthy families who usually earned their living by collecting rents from their tenant farmers, practicing medicine only as a sideline, as a way perhaps of achieving self-fulfillment. Naomichi, he recalled, used to boast that his family lineage could be traced to the famous Kusunokis of the fourteenth century. But the Hanaokas of Nate were at first just humble farmers who did not become even part-time doctors until much later. Naomichi's father had been the first to practice medicine exclusively. Yet this family was too far beneath the Imoses to get their daughter.

Finally he addressed his wife. "You may be quite right about

Otsugi, but Naomichi remains a problem. I remember how he negotiated with the Matsumotos for his bride, taking advantage of their very sick young daughter. I'll bet he prodded Otsugi into coming here. Maybe it's a Hanaoka tradition to get a wife from a prosperous family. Well, I won't go along with it."

Sajihei was having great difficulty shedding his doubts. But his wife persisted. From the decisive manner in which she expressed herself, it was apparent that she, too, had mulled the matter over.

"Why not ask the Hanaokas to accept Kae without a dowry? It's been said that Otsugi didn't bring one. Maybe the Matsumotos only furnished her wardrobe. Just look at Naomichi's old house. It's shabbier than ever!"

Before Sajihei could answer, Tami intruded and excused herself for the interruption. "I know it's impertinent, but I must tell you something. Last night I asked Kae what was bothering her because she looked so upset. Well, she wouldn't tell me. But I think she's anxious to marry into the Hanaoka family."

The surprised parents asked Tami how Kae happened to learn about the proposal, and to this the maid replied without embarrassment, "Walls have ears."

"Does Kae know Umpei?" inquired an increasingly worried Sajihei. If his daughter had fallen in love he could never condone such promiscuity.

"No, she has never seen the man," said Tami, shaking her head. "My mistress has been in love with the beautiful woman who visited yesterday. Now she's in tears . . . wishing only to become her daughter-in-law. And she didn't sleep a wink last night."

"And how did she get to know Otsugi?"

"Every woman around here knows and admires Otsugi. It's

well known that although her own family was wealthy, she doesn't complain about her present poverty. And it's because of her that the Hanaokas are liked in these parts. Kae is thrilled that Otsugi wants her, and she's afraid that she won't have any happiness if she doesn't marry Umpei."

Though Tami's interpretation might have been somewhat exaggerated, she certainly captured the essence of Kae's feelings. Sajihei was puzzled and even shaken by the maid's story. Yet his fatherly instincts still told him not to part with his daughter. Soon he became irritated with his wife for her seeming collusion with the maid.

"What makes you think Otsugi's so wonderful? Can you imagine another woman proposing such bold ideas?"

"She probably hoped to avoid any misunderstanding that might arise because of our different backgrounds. Didn't you say she implied as much?"

"Otsugi talked as though medicine were the most important thing in the world. And that's bound to be a bad omen for a healthy family like ours."

"Oh, when people get sick, they're grateful for medical care. But when they recover, they are more thankful to God than to the medicines that cured them. Not to mention how easily they forget their doctor!"

Since Grandfather's death, all of the Imoses had been in fine health, so that it was perhaps not the right time to remind Sajihei of doctors. Bearing this in mind, it was natural for him to find Otsugi's arguments about the doctor's central role in society highly overstated. His wife, however, kept on insisting that medicine was useful, necessary in emergencies, and so on.

The discussion was making Sajihei more and more uncomfortable. He sensed his wife's unhappiness in the deep sighs she let out from time to time and imagined that she must have been thinking again of the hardships she had endured in the course of their marriage. For many years she had served her in-laws, with their stuffy pride in tradition and status. She had respected ancient Imose customs and had behaved with reserve on all occasions, since there was always a precedent for her comportment. When she first came as a new bride, it had been hard for her to breathe in those rooms, filled with the gloomy spirits of the past. In a way, she had been living precisely as Otsugi had described—in a secure and serene family already well established.

She did not realize that she had been oppressing her present daughter-in-law in a similar fashion while hoping that her own daughter would have more freedom. Although she did not really know the Hanaokas, she judged from Naomichi's character and the impression she got of his small house that Kae at the very least would not be stifled. Thus, as a result of her past and the fact that her daughter's happiness was at stake, she now asserted herself rather forcefully before her husband.

"As for the bridegroom-to-be, he is Dr. Hanaoka's pride and joy. He's talked about a great deal, and many expect he'll become a good physician. His father may have certain questionable traits, but it's the son and not the father that counts this time."

"I've heard he's stupid," snapped a despondent Sajihei.

"Oh, yes. I've heard that too. There's a rumor that he once found something on a deserted road and waited almost the entire day for someone to claim the article. They also say that he never shows up for festivities no matter who invites him. And that he climbs mountains to gather weeds instead of firewood."

"Would a sensible young man do such strange things? Do you want to give Kae to an idiot?"

"Rumors are generally full of praise and abuse. You know

that Dr. Hanaoka taught his son to read and write so that Umpei did not attend the local school. How can his intelligence be fairly judged then? Some claim he's far from stupid . . . actually remarkably bright."

"In any case he must have been a peculiar child."

"I suppose there's no smoke without fire. All rumors contain a grain of truth."

"You're absolutely right."

But she did not give in. "If you agree that he's stupid and intelligent at the same time, maybe he'll become a genius. Remember he has a smart mother behind him."

Sajihei seemed momentarily at a loss for a reply. In the meantime, his wife took the opportunity to sum up her thoughts.

"I appreciate this offer simply because Kae is wanted by a woman with good judgment and great foresight."

Sajihei did not want to listen further to her opinions. Finally, as if to challenge her inclination to be grateful to the Hanaokas, he came up with an objection that he felt could not be refuted, and began to speak in a more relaxed manner.

"Isn't it funny when you think about it? The intended bridegroom has just gone off to Kyoto for at least three years according to Otsugi. But who can be sure of the length of time? And if he does return in three years, do you know how old Kae will be then? Twenty-four!"

If Umpei was not to be away indefinitely, Sajihei knew that the Hanaokas were not likely to send the bride to join her husband for the limited time remaining. Aware of his wife's concern over Kae's age, and of her desire to see her daughter married that year, he did not expect his last comment to meet with counter-objections. And in order to conclude the unexpectedly complicated matter quickly, he sent for the village headman of

Hirayama and gave him the formal answer of the Imose family for the Hanaokas.

The Hirayama headman appeared embarrassed, as if Otsugi's conduct were his responsibility, and hurried off to deliver the message. But Otsugi, unperturbed, immediately gave that same messenger a letter for the Imoses which said the following:

> With your permission we would like to have Kae before the end of the year. It would be better this way because she would have a chance to get used to life in a doctor's house and could greet Umpei as a member of the Hanaoka family upon his return. We would naturally be most happy to arrange a provisional marriage ceremony and make the appropriate announcements to the villagers.

Once again the Imoses recognized Otsugi's cleverness. In the letter, moreover, she urged them to let Kae marry without all the usual preparations for a dowry and clothing since the Hanaoka house was quite small. It seemed as though Otsugi knew exactly what was in Sajihei's mind.

Largely owing to Kae's determination, the intricacies were eventually resolved, and it was agreed that the Imoses and Hanaokas be united. After he learned that his daughter was neither eating nor sleeping, Sajihei had to change his original stance, which had been to ignore Otsugi no matter what she said. Not that Kae fasted as a way of protesting to her parents; it was simply a case where tension and disappointment caused her stomach to reject all foods, even a rice dish that she especially liked. Besides indigestion, she had severe chest pains and could not fall asleep, all of which made Tami worry about her.

One night, Kae had a vision of a brightly illuminated path unfolding before her, and at the end stood Otsugi like a goddess close to the gates of paradise. After many years under the sheltered Imose roof, she was suddenly full of excitement. But it didn't last. In an instant the gleam was extinguished, the path faded, and she found herself in the darkness of her room. Though she did not try to extract a profound meaning from the dream, the memory of the shining light left her quite distressed. Kae did not go so far as to blame her parents for her condition, but it was apparent that she was in a state of shock.

Otsugi had counted on Kae to be in satisfactory health. But to everyone's dismay, she was getting extremely thin. It may be that her rather childish behavior and naive attitudes were a consequence of the protected life she had enjoyed in the strict samurai household. Now, at the first crossroads of womanhood, she was still possessed by Otsugi's beauty. The bridegroom, Umpei, never came into her deliberations.

IV

In the fall of 1782, the Imoses held a lavish farewell party for their daughter who was about to set off to get married. Afterwards, in accordance with local custom, Kae, wearing a white cotton veil and elegant bridal kimono, was carried to Hirayama in a palanquin, unaccompanied by her family.

Upon her arrival, the lovely bride walked alone into the house, whereupon she was warmly greeted by an eager and impatient Otsugi, who led her by the hand into the main room. There a special cushion awaited her. The ceremony which was about to begin would have to take place without the groom, who had gone to Kyoto more than half a year before. (A biography of Hanaoka Seishu that was later compiled indicates some ambiguity concerning the date of his marriage, due undoubtedly to these circumstances.) Was such an arrangement commonplace? Indeed it was rare. But it never provoked any sort of criticism when it occurred. Also, as long as the groom intended to return, his absence at the wedding did not jeopardize the bride's place in her new family. For Kae this would not have been a problem anyway because everything had been planned by her future mother-in-law.

Instead of Umpei, a famous book entitled *Honzo Komoku* graced the groom's seat. Actually, it was a precious manuscript, painstakingly copied by hand with delicate brushstrokes. Originally written by Li Shih-chen of the Ming dynasty, it was considered the Chinese bible of herbal remedies. Umpei's grandfather, Hanaoka Unsen Naomasa, had copied it when he was still a student. Ever since Unsen, the Hanaokas had been practicing medicine to the exclusion of other occupations, which explains *Honzo Komoku*'s particular significance for this family. Three generation of Hanaokas—Unsen, his son Naomichi, and now Umpei—had thoroughly absorbed its contents, as verified by its old paper, faded ink, and worn cover. Appearing at the wedding banquet, the venerable text, speechless as it was, seemed to have a presence of its own and repeatedly reminded Kae that hereafter she would be a member of a family dedicated to medicine.

Having just arrived from the crowded gathering at the Imoses, Kae now felt alone and began to tremble before the Hanaokas—Naomichi, Otsugi, and some of Umpei's brothers and sisters. One brother had undertaken an apprenticeship in the merchant's guild, an opportunity that arose through the assistance of the Matsumotos; another had recently entered the priesthood. Five other children were also present: Okatsu, the same age as Kae, Koriku, two years younger, two smaller sisters, and three-year-old Ryohei. Kae could scarcely distinguish their faces through the veil covering her own.

With great dignity Otsugi stood up and lifted Kae's veil. Shimomura Ryoan, the assistant to Naomichi, began to pour cold saké into each antique, deep vermilion, lacquered cup. As Kae watched the saké reach the brim, thoughts of her new life raced through her mind. One consideration dominated the rest. If this drink would truly join her to the family, then by all means she had to swallow it quickly. Looking up, she noticed Otsugi holding her own cup and gazing at her with gentle, smiling eyes that seemed to whisper, "Everything will be all right. Just drink the saké. We have all been waiting for this day." Although Kae found this expression of affection embarrassing, she felt reassured and hurriedly pressed the cup to her lips to conceal a surge of tears. Except for a spiced saké that she had been permitted to drink at New Year celebrations, she had never tasted alcohol. Gradually, the cold liquid felt warmer as it slipped down her throat, and she heaved a sigh of relief. Then, realizing that it was too soon to breathe so freely in a house where she was yet a stranger, she blushed a deep red.

The austerity of their lives was demonstrated by the dinner that ensued. It consisted of just two dishes, one of which was the festive red bean rice. Not even a whole fish was included! Naomichi, however, was treated to two bottles of saké. Of course, this meal could in no way compare to the one that had been served at the Imoses, where forty guests had attended a magnificent feast. There every person had received his own tray with four entrées along with an additional side tray. At the Hanaokas, Okatsu and Otsugi each returned only once to the kitchen for second helpings.

Kae listened to her father-in-law, a bit drunk, recite his family genealogy starting with Emperor Bitatsu. While he talked, she felt a growing sense of fulfillment which she compared with the emptiness that had gripped her earlier at the Imoses. She naturally did not take into account the fact that a new family was exciting, whereas her own was very familiar.

Naomichi's recollections soon reached the origins of his family name.

According to him, the Hanaokas had been so named since a certain Wada Goro chose to live in the village of Hanaoka in Kawachi province, near Osaka. Meanwhile, Okatsu and Koriku began to clear the table. It made Kae uncomfortable to watch them work, but Otsugi rejected her offer to help and motioned for her to remain seated.

"Please stay right where you are, next to the groom's place, and listen to your father-in-law. The climax is coming. From Wada Goro to himself there are six generations. All of us know this history quite well, but it's your first time. Don't worry if you can't remember the small details. You'll have many chances to hear them again."

Otsugi smiled and even Okatsu and Koriku grinned when their mother mentioned the frequency with which Kae would hear their father's favorite story. Giggling, they disappeared into the kitchen. The incident, however, assuaged Kae's nervousness, and she was grateful for Otsugi's thoughtfulness.

The graying hair on Naomichi's forehead had receded considerably, and his topknot had been casually tied and was off-center, an indication of how little he cared about his appearance. In spite of a concentration of wrinkles around the eyes, the reddish skin from his high cheekbones to his chin looked healthy. He was certainly a robust figure of a man in his striped cotton kimono and short jacket, which bore huge white paulownia crests that were odd—amusingly echoing his size. His attire contrasted sharply with his wife's, who as usual was properly and tastefully dressed. Kae did not listen to him because she felt obliged to learn the family history; she was truly fascinated with his long narration, which revealed above all the extraordinary ambition and drive for perfection that

characterized his family. Under the influence of the saké, Naomichi expounded effusively on the subject, although he seemed
to be more intoxicated by his own voice than by the bottle.

"Any way you look at it, a doctor's duty is to save human
life. The loss of a single patient fills me with remorse and
sadness, even in those cases where death is caused by old age.
Naturally, a doctor must not show his feelings on his face. It
wouldn't be good for his practice. . . . Now, where was I?
Oh, yes. Starting way back with Denemon Naochika, who
only gave part of his time to medicine, I am the second generation and Umpei will be the third to devote all of his
energies to it. Of course, our past is full of mistakes, dark as
compost, for which we have many regrets. Yet no one in our
family can be accused of having used medicine for personal
gain. I know some people make fun of me. They think I brag
too much about Umpei. But the fact is that I don't think of him
as just *my* son. I'm convinced that the time has come for the
Hanaoka tree to bear *real* fruits. And I believe Umpei is the
very reincarnation of the desires and dreams of my ancestors,
who wished for something marvelous to be accomplished by
our family. As descendants of samurai who had abandoned the
sword, we weren't really satisfied when we took up the plow.
And I think we've preferred to help our fellowman with a
spoon. Well, we sent our third son to Mt. Koya to study for
the priesthood so that he might pray for those who have died
because of our lack of skill or just plain bad luck. It takes about
one hundred years of evolution to create a great man, and the
Hanaokas have been involved with medicine for nearly a century. So, our destiny is perhaps ready to manifest itself. My son
Umpei shall be that great man."

The kitchen all tidied, the sisters quietly joined the others in
the main room. Everyone was listening to Naomichi—Otsugi,

33

Okatsu, Koriku, and the little girls—and all nodded in appreciation despite their familiarity with the tale. Kae admired their attentiveness and the way in which they seemed unanimously to share Naomichi's convictions. She was also impressed by Naomichi, though she knew he was mocked for his boasting. A sense of pride was developing in her as he spoke because the glorious hero of the narrative was her own husband; and she began to wonder to what seat of honor Otsugi had invited her.

Naomichi chatted until midnight. "Long ago," he was saying, "before Umpei was born, I had ideas for my son's future. I made up my mind to look for a wise, beautiful woman to bear my children, which explains my frantic determination when I discovered Otsugi's predicament."

Kae cast a stealthy glance in Otsugi's direction, but she was concentrating on Naomichi without the least sign of embarrassment—like a believer intent on the words of a virtuous priest. It suddenly occurred to Kae that she might have been pursued by the Hanaokas for the same reasons that Naomichi had sought Otsugi. A surge of joy such as she had not felt for some time caused her to shiver as she perceived her function in the Hanaoka genealogy.

"Twenty-three years ago Umpei was born." The story, which was probably being repeated for the hundredth time, advanced. Kae remembered much of it when it had been told to her grandfather, yet on this night everything sounded different. Naomichi also added a description of Otsugi's labor, for he felt free to speak about this in his own home. "Otsugi started to pant. She looked as though she was in terrible pain, and I couldn't bear to watch her. I stared into the garden and noticed what a fine day it was. Not a patch of cloud in the sky! As I thought about putting some herbal leaves out to dry in the sun, I recalled a premonition I had had about

34

the Hanaoka heir, namely, that he would be born only on such a beautiful day. So I decided not to bother with the leaves. Otsugi soon went into labor. She sweated and groaned. I shouted, 'Boil some water. Get the midwife!' Then a downpour of heavy rain struck the earth and a streak of lightning zigzagged across the darkened sky. Thunder roared nearby, shaking the ground under Mt. Katsuragi. I held Otsugi tightly and told her to have courage. The midwife didn't arrive because of the storm, so I delivered Umpei myself. I still remember his first sounds." He gestured to show how he cradled the baby, and then tried to stifle the emotion that had overtaken him at the memory. "Otsugi gave birth to seven more children, but I only delivered that one. What a loud cry came out of that baby! All of a sudden I noticed that the sky had cleared. Once again the autumn day was unbelievably beautiful. I was convinced that this child was the one the Hanaokas had been waiting for. When I finished bathing him, the midwife appeared, and I let her take care of the rest. I then walked in the garden and saw a white cloud float calmly by, as if nothing had happened. It was at that moment that I thought of the perfect name for the child. Umpei, 'the peaceful cloud.' A marvelous name, isn't it?"

After so many repetitions some magnification was natural. Kae had been visualizing her mother-in-law while he spoke, how she must have been feeling contented and peaceful after the birth of the much desired male child. She also observed that Otsugi was watching her husband with a tender, mellow expression of happiness. Kae wondered if she ever became bored with the description of Umpei's arrival in the world.

"Shall we end this evening now that the bridegroom has been successfully born?" inquired Otsugi in a tone that cleverly managed to bring Naomichi's interminable tale to a close.

Kae entered a small room which also served as sleeping quarters for the women. With the help of Okatsu and Koriku who brought her some water, she washed her face. Neither girl had the delicate features or vivacious spirit of their mother. They were both "silent" types and this, combined with Kae's timidity, made for a certain awkwardness. Kae, accustomed to being looked after by Tami, did not really know how to respond to the kindness of her sisters-in-law, and felt uneasy while they waited on her. However, there was little she could do for herself in these strange surroundings. As she began to put away her bridal kimono, she thought of her mother and realized that she had never been told anything special about her own birth—probably because nothing spectacular had occurred on that day. Even so, she missed her. She recalled that although the wedding date had been hastily set, her mother had carefully planned her bridal costume. Everyone at the Imoses had admired its beauty, yet no one had commented on it in this house. Her mother would surely have been disappointed at the lack of attention. But Kae had no complaints, because she was at last with the family for which she had been longing. Handling the kimono, she knew for the first time that her own house was very far away.

In the next room Ryohei began to cry. He must have been awakened by his sisters, who had been wandering in and out rather often. "I want to see the bride," he sobbed. With the white veil covering her face and the splendid kimono, Kae must have made quite an impression on the child before he went to bed. His sisters tried to soothe him, but he didn't stop crying. Finally his mother quieted him by promising that he could sleep near the bride, and holding his hand, she brought him to Kae.

"Now here's the bride of your big brother, your new sister-in-law, Ryohei."

Ryohei stared at Kae in disbelief, for she had changed into her nightgown. Unlike his sisters, he strongly resembled his mother, especially around the eyes and mouth. Kae tried to think how she could help the perplexed child understand that she was the same person of a few hours earlier. And in an instant she spread her bridal kimono before him.

"So beautiful, isn't it, Mother?" exclaimed the joyful boy.

His honest and innocent admiration evoked a short, "Indeed it is," from his mother, and Kae felt that her costume had at last achieved recognition.

That night Kae and Otsugi slept in the same room. Ryohei lay beside his mother with his hand at her bosom as if to embrace her. Kae tucked her wooden pillow gently under her neck and wondered which of the parents, Naomichi or Otsugi, Umpei resembled. The virgin bride felt neither estranged nor unhappy sleeping next to her mother-in-law on her wedding night. On the contrary, she was completely tranquil and ready for pleasant dreams.

V

The normal routine resumed the day after the wedding. Okatsu and Koriku did the cooking and laundry under their mother's supervision while the maid cleaned and cared for the younger children. Shimomura Ryoan performed various duties for the doctor since the women and children were not allowed to so much as touch the drawers containing medical supplies. Little time, however, was required to prepare the simple meals and straighten up the small house, so that most of the daily tasks were quickly completed. Now, the Hanaokas kept some looms on the veranda and a spinning wheel in a nearby storage area. When their chores were done, the older girls, skilled at weaving, went off and worked at the looms without a break until dinner. Their special weave used dyed threads that Kae surmised must have come from the Matsumotos.

At first Kae thought the sisters were making clothes for their future marriages. Tami had once told her that a farmer's daughter had to put together her own wardrobe, after which any extra fabrics she had were sold to get money for her dowry. "They may need silk garments," Kae wondered, and considered giving them some of hers.

But she soon discovered that they were not working for their own interests. Every so often a merchant from across the river collected finished rolls of cloth from each house in Hirayama which he sold to the city dwellers of Sakai. On his return trip he brought his village suppliers either cash or merchandise. Kae observed that the Hanaokas never sought remuneration in the form of goods for the girls. They asked only for money, which Otsugi saved until she had a certain sum. The entire amount was then sent to Umpei through another vendor or through someone at the dye works who was planning to go to Kyoto on business.

When Kae found out where the money was going, she felt compelled to get Otsugi's permission to weave. Her request was readily granted. After giving her a detailed lesson on operating the shuttle, her mother-in-law warned her not to hurry or the threads would tangle.

The loom was absolutely new to her, but it did not take Kae long to match her sisters-in-law in skill. With no sisters of her own, she appreciated their kindness toward her as she sat weaving to the gay "click-clack" of the loom. Okatsu, she noticed, resembled her mother in character, intelligence, and common sense, while Koriku was quieter and tended to follow her sister's instructions. Kae worked hard to show her gratitude, and was soon producing at least five inches of cloth every day. Her natural dexterity and knowledge of embroidery encouraged her to rearrange the threads, so that after a while she was creating original, imaginative patterns. The sisters admired them, though neither was interested in deviating from her fixed way: Okatsu continued weaving striped cloth, Koriku cloth of one color. And Kae was happy just the same. It seemed that she had truly become accepted into the family. Gone were those days when she felt insecure and didn't know what to say or how to act. She also enjoyed the flattery of the merchants who spoke of her popularity in the markets of Sakai. But above all, it was Otsugi's appreciation, encouragement, and continual praises—bestowed even in the presence of visitors—that thrilled her.

"Please, look at this elegant striped pattern over here," Otsugi would say. "Marvelous, isn't it? Though Kae was not brought up to work hard, she has truly pitched in to help our family. Umpei will be very proud to have such a fine wife."

The bright fashions she was accustomed to wearing, and to some extent her embroideries, had taught Kae something about coordinating colors. On the whole the merchants shared Otsugi's enthusiasm for her patterns, but from a strictly professional point of view, they probably did not regard them as quite so spectacular. Kae herself realized that her designs were not exceptional; besides which, the fabrics were only of cotton. Yet she was extremely pleased to see Otsugi contented with her. Every day she tried to increase her production because she felt her feelings were reciprocated by her mother-in-law. On the surface she seemed oblivious to the yearning for her unseen husband that was beginning to possess her. Still, any mention of Umpei gained her undivided attention, and once back at the loom, she would recall the smallest detail of those conversations about him. But the virgin wife had no inkling of her growing love, and would not have been able to acknowledge that it was motivating her imagination and inspiring the bold, fanciful designs in her fabrics.

Umpei never wrote a single letter to Kae, nor did he ever

thank his family for the money. Naomichi himself rarely heard from him and had to learn to accept the situation. "No news is good news," he used to say patiently. "If one is concentrating on an education, there's no time to think of home." But despite his humor and affable nature, shadows of loneliness often crossed his face.

From his past experiences away from Hirayama, Naomichi knew that living in the city was expensive and difficult on a student's budget. Therefore, he turned over every cent he earned to his wife and instructed her to send all of it to his son. On his sixtieth birthday he was still an energetic talker, but it was apparent shortly afterwards that old age was creeping up on him. When he began to have trouble making house visits, his assistant Ryoan had to take over those calls. Naomichi saw patients just at his home. As was customary for country doctors, he treated every ailment, from colds and minor lacerations to broken bones and severe illnesses. But, since dermatology was known to be his specialty, many suffering from all kinds of skin maladies came to him. The groans and anguished cries that emanated from the examination room frightened Kae and gave her nightmares, though after a year she became somewhat accustomed to them. Still the screams often interrupted her work, and occasionally she had images of seeping bandages or blood splattering from the surgical removal of a wart. The realities that confronted her were equally unpleasant: children covered with scabs, women whose skin had been affected by improper medication, and so on, all of them waiting for Naomichi in the reception area. When she saw these helpless unfortunates, she sometimes recalled how Naomichi had cured his wife. Yet she was inclined to believe that it was Otsugi's intrinsic beauty alone that eventually expelled the sickness from her body, not Naomichi's expertise!

Their financial circumstances grew worse. Marriage preparations for Okatsu and Koriku (if there had been any) and Naomichi's habitual drink at dinner were suspended. Sometimes the almost destitute family subsisted on just potatoes and rice porridge for several days. Nor was there always money to purchase medical supplies. But, despite adversity, the Hanaokas neither acted as though they were poor nor appeared dejected. Each and every member pinned his hopes on Umpei and his success in Kyoto. Their sense of optimism was further reinforced by Otsugi's gaiety and beauty. Naomichi, Okatsu, Koriku, and now Kae labored, indeed redoubled their efforts for Umpei out of respect for Otsugi's determination, leadership, and comportment, which were all above criticism.

Kae soon became so absorbed with her patterns that she began to neglect herself entirely. Otsugi, on the other hand, who was always well dressed, neatly groomed, and sure of herself, displayed perfect physical movements and mannerisms like the graceful dancers in the Noh dramas. It seemed that however early Kae awoke, her mother-in-law had already finished her coiffure. Kae tried to discover if Otsugi had any special secrets, but found none, except perhaps that she rose before dawn and carefully pressed her kimono under her mattress every night. Also, she used a new rice bran bag to scrub herself every night when she took a bath. Kae knew it would have been hopeless had she tried to imitate her for even a single day. The more she observed Otsugi working at her appearance, the more she admired her, realizing at the same time that any such effort was beyond her.

Nor could Okatsu and Koriku compete with their mother. Both of them seemed content to use Otsugi's discarded rice bran bag for their baths. Eventually Kae did so too. Kae noticed that the bags sometimes contained dark brown sugar and nightingale droppings, which was an indication that Otsugi was taking extra care to maintain her fresh and youthful complexion. Of course, Kae never imagined that she would become beautiful by simply washing herself with Otsugi's cleansers. Yet, when she rubbed Otsugi's silk bran bag against her body, she felt at least then that her skin was fairer and smoother. Later, she would hang that same wet bag out to dry under the eaves of the roof.

Otsugi took care of her person and clothing in so many different ways. For example, before sweeping, she covered her hair with a towel, tied her sleeves back and rolled up the hem of her kimono. Or, when pulling out weeds, she wore special gloves. And it was amazing to watch her water the plants; she managed never to splash even a drop of water on herself.

Once in a while Kae offered to help her in the garden. With a patience and indulgence that surpassed that of Kae's own mother, Otsugi taught her about plants, and how to distinguish those that could be used in medicines. Kae watched and tried to get acquainted with the many varieties of foliage. Since the wedding night the two women had been sharing the same room, so Kae no longer felt restrained and awkward in her presence. Whenever she tired of weaving, it was a welcome change for her to step into the autumn sunshine and squat beside her mother-in-law. Naturally, she never bothered to protect her hands.

"What good is that Crazy Eggplant?" asked Kae one day.

"Which one? . . . That purple-green plant? Oh, do you call that Crazy Eggplant? Across the river where I come from, this is named Korean Morning Glory because of its shape. I remember carpets of them along the river."

"Korean Morning Glory! What a lovely name!" Kae was ashamed that she had not known it.

By the end of summer the Korean Morning Glories had lost their blossoms and had borne reddish purple fruits, the size of a child's fist. These plants, with their prickly thorns hidden among the leaves, grew tenaciously even in the worst soil conditions.

"My husband and Ryoan call them *mandarage*," said Otsugi. "We've been warned about putting it near our mouths because of its strong poison. They say that if you taste it, you'll laugh yourself to death. Maybe Crazy Eggplant is the right name."

The leaves of this plant were dried, mixed with tobacco, and used in treating asthma or as an anesthetic. While Kae was pulling weeds, she suddenly remembered the day she saw Otsugi for the first time.

"I saw these flowers when I came here once before. They were so white and beautiful."

"When was that?"

"When I was eight years old."

"Did you really come to this house so long ago? I wonder why I have no recollection of your visit."

Otsugi must have mistakenly thought that Kae had been brought to Naomichi as a patient. Puzzled because she could not recall her, Otsugi stopped weeding for a moment and looked at Kae.

"I came here to spy on you."

"To spy?"

"Yes, Mother. When my nurse told me the story of how you came to live in Hirayama, I begged her to let me see the beautiful woman for myself. Please forgive me."

Otsugi's gay laughter at her apology made Kae laugh as well. Then Otsugi spoke more softly. "I am called 'Mother' by you though you are not really my child. Yet I feel you are as dear to me as my own daughters. Our relationship has deep roots. It was probably decreed by fate."

Kae nodded and believed that the two had been destined to become mother and daughter from a former life.

VI

The excessive rainfall of the previous year had destroyed many crops throughout the country, and now, early in the spring, it began to rain again. The winters in the Kishu region are relatively mild, so the only heating in the houses comes from a kitchen fireplace. Since the weavers worked on the veranda, they were sheltered from the rain but not from the winds, cold air, and drafts. After prolonged exposure to these conditions, several of Kae's fingers, already colored by a blue dye in the threads, became severely chapped and had to be treated with the family's special ointment and bandaged. Weaving was now difficult for her; the shuttle often dropped out of her hands and threads snapped repeatedly. Her sisters-in-law, seemingly unaffected by the dampness and the chilly temperature, carried on to the monotonous "click-clack" of their looms.

One morning, so dark and frosty she could not believe it was the end of winter, Kae wondered if she were physically ill. By noon, the sight of the broken threads made Kae too irritated to concentrate on her pattern. Suddenly she heard a loud voice coming from the front entrance. Thinking it was her father-in-law's, she failed to notice that Okatsu had stopped her loom and Koriku practically stood with the shuttle still in her hand.

"Oh, it must be Brother! It must be!" cried the girls in unison as they rushed from the room. Realizing that her husband had returned at last, Kae also headed in the same direction—without bothering to tidy her hair.

Umpei was soon surrounded by his mother and sisters.

"Welcome home."

"You look good."

"We didn't expect you back yet."

Like a festive chorus, the women spoke all at once. And Umpei, with one wicker basket on his back and another in his hand, was standing speechless and quite drenched in his straw raincoat, though he didn't seem chilled—having perhaps grown accustomed to the rain on his long walk home.

"You should soak your feet in warm water," suggested Otsugi. Then, noticing Kae in the background, she gave her a quick, piercing look. The smile she wore when she turned back to her son was apparently contrived.

"This is Kae. She has also been waiting for you."

Umpei nodded, and his large, sparkling eyes focused directly on Kae's face without any of the shyness or embarrassment typical of young people. But he could not think of a proper greeting for this woman, his wife whom he had never met, and he barely managed to open his mouth and utter a short, senseless sound. And his wife, equally overwhelmed, could do no more than bow and hurry off to the kitchen with the excuse of fetching some boiling water from the stove.

Kae found a wooden pail, filled it at the well, scampered to the kitchen to add some hot water, took an extra empty basin and hurried back to Umpei. But he had finished wiping his feet with a towel handed him by his sister and was already inside the house when Kae appeared holding the pail.

"Oh, he's finished, thank you." The curt tone contrasted sharply with Otsugi's smiling face as she pushed Umpei forward to where the arthritic and almost incapacitated Naomichi awaited his son.

A despondent Kae, feeling alone and that she did not belong, remained rooted to the floor. "What sort of homecoming is this?" she asked herself. "I'm Umpei's wife. But he went right by me to see his father." After a while she walked slowly toward the well, emptied the water and watched the steam rise in the chilly air.

The feeling of being excluded followed her to the kitchen. She had counted on cooking her husband's first dinner at home until she saw Okatsu and Koriku happily engaged in a discussion of their brother's favorite foods.

"Let's cut up lots of turnips."

"All right. Umpei loves them."

How could a new wife compete with them? What would she know of Umpei's tastes? Their conversation, reflecting the twenty years of experiences they had shared with their brother, made Kae feel like a nuisance in the kitchen, although she hesitated to join the others in Naomichi's room. Was she being overly sensitive? Still, even thoughtful, gentle Otsugi seemed cold and distant to her on this special day. Over and over she kept asking herself what in the world she meant to this family. She admitted that in the beginning Umpei had not occupied an important place in her heart. But now that his presence was real, he looked like the husband for whom she had been longing. And she could not help thinking that the Hanaokas were heartless, and were interfering in her long-imagined meeting with her beloved.

She began to contemplate the physical attributes of her twenty-six-year-old husband, just two years older than herself. With big, penetrating eyes and bushy eyebrows, he was of medium height, had an unusually large head, and a short, thick stubble covered his unshaven face. Clearly, only six-year-old Ryohei had inherited his mother's beautiful features. In her imagination Kae had fashioned an oval-faced, handsome man. But again her expectations did not materialize. Yet, despite her disappointments and unhappiness, she felt close to Umpei. Strange as this eruption of sentiment might seem in view of the past, Kae reasoned that it was perfectly natural for a wife to feel warmth for her husband in his presence.

Almost everyone felt cheerful that night at dinner. Naomichi got out of bed and joined the family, sitting opposite Umpei at the table. Ryoan and Imose Yonejiro, a relative of Kae's who had become Naomichi's assistant over a year before, were also there and anxious to hear about Kyoto. It was soon apparent that the food would not be as important as the stories of the loquacious young doctor. As for Kae, her attention was drawn to a black mole on the left side of Umpei's throat beneath his chin, which seemed to move up and down when he spoke.

"Dr. Yamato taught the same surgical procedures as the old Dutch physician, Caspar. All the instruments I've brought with me come from Holland. Some, I'm sure, will even impress you, Father. They're quite different from your Spanish ones."

"Well, both Dr. Yamato and his former teacher Dr. Kensui claim that for a successful operation the surgeon must consider every aspect of his patient's anatomy and not merely the local symptoms in the problem area. The idea is to search for basic causes, which after all is what makes medicine a science. In order to gain a broader perspective, I also studied under Dr. Yoshimasu, a Chinese specialist."

After a short pause he resumed. "But you know, Father, I owe a good deal of my ability and insights to the observations I made when I watched you. It's true you were trained to be a surgeon, but as a village practitioner, you had to treat all kinds of illness, including colds. I came to understand that most cases cannot be diagnosed with absolute accuracy. It was often not clear which needed surgery and which might have responded better to medicine. I've decided that I can improve present surgical procedures if I implement Caspar's ideas and techniques and Yoshimasu's broad practical knowledge of the human body. You see, one of my goals is to discover the laws of nature by making objective studies."

"To discover the laws of nature by making objective studies," repeated his father slowly. "Indeed!"

Umpei pursued the idea. "The Dutch and the Chinese each have positive and negative qualities. It happens that some students have absorbed only the Dutch approach and can reason and deal well with abstractions. But they hardly understand how the body actually works because they lack experimental training. On the other hand, students of Chinese medicine know many details about the body but cannot translate their knowledge into cause and effect, which of course makes them ridiculous in the eyes of the Dutch advocates. The fact is a good doctor ought to be able to draw logical conclusions from his diagnoses and understand how the body functions at the same time."

"Indeed," agreed his father.

"The real surgical expert is the one who has some familiarity with medicine. Knowing how to remove a tumor is not enough. A surgeon, in fact, should only take the patient whom a doctor can't cure, which means that the knife is used as a last resort—like the samurai's sword, if you like, as an arbiter distinguishing between the reasonable and the unreasonable. And the knife must never be used under any circumstance until a complete diagnosis has been made."

"Well spoken, Umpei!"

"Wisdom is the most valuable asset a doctor can have. Not to be a follower of old or new fashions, that's essential!" His ideas and feelings poured out with great exuberance. "It's time to call the surgeon when a specific medicine, acupuncture, or moxibustion all fail. Between you and me, he's like the star of Kabuki who appears on stage to give the final scene, a role I find deeply satisfying. In fact, I would like to be the Hua Tu of Japan."

"You don't mean the Chinese Hua Tu?" inquired his father. "That's quite a man you picked." Accustomed to being labeled a braggart, Naomichi was astonished to hear Umpei boast in such a brash manner. To wish to be compared with that famous skilled doctor who lived nearly sixteen hundred years ago! Naomichi's eyes widened and he repeated the name. The facial expressions of father and son were often very similar.

"Yes, the same Hua Tu," asserted the self-confident, ambitious young man. "My education in Kyoto was just the beginning. Of course, the acquisition of new information and remarkable abilities to diagnose correctly earned my deep respect for Yamato and Yoshimasu. But they're no match for Hua Tu. There are illnesses that remain an incurable enigma to Westerners and Orientals alike. Cancer, for example, especially of the breast, where the malignancy can't be removed by surgery because it's believed the breast is vital for a woman. In this situation a surgeon is completely helpless."

"It's a real problem," agreed Naomichi.

"But Hua Tu not only removed tumors from the skull, he opened up the chest cavity and sewed it together again. Maybe he owed his successes to an anesthetic of hot narcotic water which he is said to have used to induce sleep. Isn't it a shame there are no records of either this anesthetic or the operations themselves? What's your opinion, Father?"

"Naturally, it's a pity. But portions of these stories about him might have been pure invention. After all, he lived nearly two thousand years ago and Chinese literature of that period is full of exaggerated descriptions."

"That's so. Yet I don't think the whole legend is false. Besides, if even half were true, think how terrific it would be. Imagine if a patient could sleep during an entire operation? It seems to me that without pain his physical endurance would last probably twice as long."

"Maybe more than twice," affirmed Naomichi.

"Well, that's the situation, Father. I'd like to be the one to discover a cure for some disease that has every doctor baffled. I think that means becoming a Hua Tu." He paused before adding, "The first step may be to develop an anesthetic that will allow all parts of the body to be operated upon. Then any unusual growth could be eliminated before it became malignant. Nowadays a woman would surely die if she submitted to an operation for breast cancer. But I believe there must be a solution . . . a surgical procedure . . . maybe by cutting through the underarm or from the back."

"Don't be so quick to operate," advised his father. "People expect their doctor to find other remedies."

"But suppose the person were convinced that surgery would

53

be painless? Wouldn't this diminish his fears?"

"If you could make such a thing possible, I would rest peacefully in heaven," exclaimed Naomichi, with the trace of a faint smile that indicated his age and the fact that he had transmitted his dreams to his successor. He seemed overwhelmed by Umpei's energy and found it hard to keep in step with the younger man's ambitions. So he turned to his wife.

"Look how our son has matured, Otsugi. Imagine speaking of such great discoveries!"

"As far as I can remember, from early childhood Umpei never talked about things he couldn't accomplish," said his wife with pride. "I believe Umpei's hopes will be fulfilled some day."

Umpei then opened one of his wicker baskets and displayed an assortment of Dutch-designed instruments: syringes, surgical knives of different shapes, special scissors, a spatula made of whale bone, needles, a large clamp, curved saw, probe, mirror, spray, hot iron, catheter tubes, and more. One by one he extracted his treasures while his wife looked on, admiring the slender fingers of her husband's large hands. Naomichi, who was beginning to tire, found his interest renewed in the array of instruments.

"Oh ho, what in the world is this one for?"

"You know the sulcus," explained Umpei, "the shallow furrow separating the convolutions on the surface of the brain? This is used to draw out fluid from an encysted tumor in that region."

"It's truly well made."

"These are Dutch scissors. Watch how they work."

"Do they cut well?"

"Very well."

Both Ryoan and Yonejiro leaned forward in fascination

to get a better view. Umpei must have brought the latest of everything that he imagined essential for his future work.

"No wonder he needed so much money," thought Kae. She felt a certain affinity toward those strange objects, knowing that at least some of them had been purchased with the help of her patterns.

Umpei took out a few bandages which consisted simply of rolls of narrow-striped Indian cotton cloth, and as if he had magic fingers, in an instant tightly wrapped the gauze around Yonejiro's right arm, covering him from the elbow to the wrist.

"No matter how you move or shake, that bandage won't come loose," the young doctor stated with satisfaction.

Yonejiro was amazed to find that he could turn his wrist and elbow in any direction, and demonstrated before Ryoan how easily he could bend and stretch his arm. Impressed by Umpei's superior method of bandaging, his companion seemed to be thinking that the long wait for the return of his master's son had been worthwhile.

"We can weave such cottons," Okatsu told her brother.

"Good. Make a lot. I need them all the time."

"Okatsu and Koriku have become excellent weavers," added Otsugi tenderly. "Your sisters have really been laboring these last three years to support your studies."

"Your sisters?" wondered Kae, not believing she had heard correctly. It wasn't just Okatsu and Koriku who sat at the loom day in and day out. What about me? Didn't I work at those stripes? Didn't Otsugi herself praise my work in front of those merchants? Why am I excluded from her acknowledgment now? No explanation appeared to satisfy her. She threw her mother-in-law a bitter glance.

Otsugi had always been careful in the past to include Kae in all conversations. But her unusual behavior tonight cast doubt as to whether she truly cared about her daughter-in-law's feelings. And since Kae had grown accustomed to thinking of herself as another daughter in the family, it was especially painful and perplexing for her to be confronted with another reality so suddenly.

"Please look at this, Father," interjected Umpei. He withdrew a piece of paper in the form of a letter which had been written in beautiful brushstrokes. Naomichi carefully scrutinized it before commenting on the author's signature:

"Signed by Asakura Keizan (Haku). . . . Is that the famous Confucian scholar who dedicated this farewell to you?"

"Yes. Please look here. Hakugyo is *my* pen name." Umpei pointed to the last section, whereupon Naomichi began to read aloud:

> Whenever you try where others have failed or have given up, you are bound to succeed. They say: "Let not Hakugyo return home, for should he practice in the capital, he would surely succeed in his profession." Hakugyo's talents are greatly appreciated here. But last February, due to his father's old age, he expressed an obligation to return to his village and asked me to write something. Now this is my belief: "Your energy surpasses that of any man, and your ambition is strong. I predict you will be well known for your outstanding achievements in the future."

"Well, well," sighed Naomichi. Asakura's document describing Umpei in Kyoto helped to account for those three years in which his son had never written to him. The first-born, sent to Kyoto by him and his wife, was home and a true physician, his excellence exceeding all expectation. "This night has been worth waiting for, hasn't it Otsugi? Now I can die any time."

Umpei laughed and rolled up the scroll. "Father, don't joke like that. I intend to be a real doctor. But, as I said, Kyoto was only the beginning. I have to investigate further if I'm to become the surgeon who will perform operations where others have failed. There's an experiment I have in mind to set up right away. So, you see, I'm not going to replace you. In fact, I'd prefer to be your dependent for a while yet. Father, you must continue to care for your patients."

"Oh no," replied the old man. "As you see, I'm terribly exhausted. Lately I've been so helpless that Ryoan has had to take charge of my patients. I've barely been able to hold out. My time is up. You may take down the sign 'Western style'; clearly Caspar's techniques supersede mine. Those instruments tell me that." Naomichi concluded on a rather dismal note which his wife lightly dismissed.

"Father is very tired. This long spell of rain has depressed everybody. Go to sleep, Umpei. It's late. By tomorrow Father will be feeling much better, and I'm sure he'll tell you that he can't retire. We'd like to hear more, but we'll have to postpone that pleasure."

"All right, Mother. I wanted to bring all of you souvenirs from Kyoto, but I spent my last cent on this curved knife. Really, I feel terrible coming home empty-handed."

"Now don't be silly. Your instruments are for all of us. They are truly the best presents. Besides, nobody expected gifts from you. Well, plenty of rest is the best cure after a long journey, although I'm not sure what Caspar would say. Tonight you ought to have a sound sleep by yourself."

The family laughed at Otsugi's joke and each person retired to his own quarters. Kae also went into her room and prepared the beds for her mother-in-law and herself. She wondered what Otsugi meant by telling Umpei to sleep alone. Didn't it imply that she was not invited to be near him?

Okatsu and Koriku arranged their brother's bed in Naomichi's room and went off to sleep. Otsugi, however, lingered near her son and showed no inclination to leave. In the silence of the night her low-pitched tittering could be heard from where Kae sat on her cold bed. It was certainly the laughter of a happy mother who could not restrain her joy on the return of her dearest son. But to Kae the sounds were lascivious.

At that moment Kae conceived an intense hatred for Otsugi. What caused the deep surge of emotions was not clear, even to her. It may have been her awareness that she still did not belong among the Hanaokas in spite of the ceremonial saké drunk three years ago; or the realization that the bonds uniting Naomichi and Otsugi were stronger than those between any husband and wife. They were linked by ties to their children and by their children's kinship to one another. But the situation Kae found herself in is common to every woman who moves into a new family and tries to break down the barriers of blood relationships, and did not cause her to despair. In fact, burning with jealousy, she yearned to fight with the woman to whom so far she had shown only love and respect. Kae knew, of course, that it was not unusual for a bride to become the enemy of her mother-in-law. Otsugi's action, which prevented her son from being with his wife, may not have been deliberate. Yet it expressed an undeniable antagonism toward her daughter-in-law. So it came to pass that the beautiful intimacy between the two—the bride and the mother-in-law who had sought her—terminated upon the arrival of the loved one they had to share. The virgin wife who had been weaving her dreams until this very day was now ready for battle.

Presently a black shadow entered the room, quietly prepared her clothing for the next morning, and slipped into the adjacent bed. Sensing that Otsugi was trying to determine whether she was asleep, Kae stared through the darkness and knew that her mother-in-law was conscious of her gaze. Then Otsugi turned over and remained motionless. Both women spent a sleepless night, each conscious of the other's presence: the mother who wanted her son to sleep alone for as long as possible, and the wife who was learning about a mother-in-law's interference in the life of a married couple. They lay in their respective positions for many hours, tense and sensitive to one another's breathing, each careful not to betray her true feelings.

VII

Hanaoka Naomichi, known as a spirited conversationalist among his fellow villagers, died peacefully less than six months after Umpei's return. It seems that once he was assured of his son's maturity and secure future, he had no further attachments to this world. He had made no formal will, since he had perhaps accounted for all his wishes while he was alive.

It turned out that the funeral served as an occasion to present Umpei and his wife to the community. Having spent far beyond their means on Umpei's education, no one in the Hanaoka family had new clothes, nor was there money for a costly wedding reception after the funeral expenses were paid. Besides, in the past year, famine had taken its toll so that even in the rich Kishu province, most budgets were tight; any display of extravagance would have been highly improper. Although spring was over, it was still so cold and rainy that people did not change into more summery clothing. In the dark and musty Hanaoka house, the family's faces appeared drained of color.

Kae knew of the financial difficulties. Yet she clung to her belief that only Otsugi's malice prevented a wedding reception from taking place. She remembered her mother-in-law's tokens of love and solicitude during the three years prior to Umpei's homecoming, especially the day Otsugi told her that their relationship had been predestined.

After Naomichi died, Otsugi began to find subtle ways to avoid her daughter-in-law. No one noticed the change, however, since she was much too clever to torment Kae overtly. But Kae could sense her hatred even if it escaped others, and it pierced her like a dart whenever she happened to be in Otsugi's presence. Otsugi undoubtedly counted on Kae's upbringing in a samurai house, which means that she could have presumed her daughter-in-law would be too discreet to protest openly or reveal her sentiments in a direct fashion.

One morning Kae sat in a corner of her room sewing her own bran bags out of remnants of red silk which she kept in a box along with some of her other belongings. As she sewed the cloth, folded double to about three inches square, with small tight stitches, she tried to provide an explanation for her past behavior. How could she have acted like a servant, using her mother-in-law's cloths, and for so long? Now that Kae had forgotten it was she herself who wanted to use Otsugi's bran bags, it was quite understandable that her hatred was directed inward for having permitted such a debasing physical intimacy. She recalled the night she first bathed with her own bag, and how it was nearly torn apart by the hard scrubbing she inflicted on her body in a fury of fierce resentment.

Otsugi suddenly hurried into the room, unaware at first of Kae's presence. But though she was soon startled to see her, she proceeded to ignore her entirely, first opening the window and then erecting a hand mirror on its stand—a gold lacquered one which looked like an expensive antique and must have come from the Matsumotos.

It was customary for Otsugi to enter the room frequently, either to fix her hair or rearrange her kimono. Usually she was quick to take out the mirror, comb her hair, return the mirror to its place, and leave. Today was different. Sitting at the opposite end of the room, she seemed to be spending an especially long time oiling her hair to the roots, an action which Kae interpreted as some kind of intentional demonstration. Obviously Otsugi was waiting for her to leave. Perhaps she wanted privacy.

The situation was truly absurd. Without any apparent falling out, the two women now rarely spoke to each another. Half a year ago, had Otsugi seen Kae sewing, she would surely have asked her what she was mending. And had Kae seen her mother-in-law set up the mirror, she would have brought out her own to help Otsugi view the back of her hair. Now the two maintained a strict silence. Each woman lingered. Neither wanted to be the first to leave.

Kae pulled out a red thread, and broke it ever so slowly with her teeth to show that she was not pressed to finish. After she completed that one cloth, she placed it in full view on the table, glancing out of the corner of her eye as she did so. The sight was unexpected and shocking. With the light streaming through the window, she was able to see many small wrinkles around Otsugi's eyes. Holding her breath, Kae hurried out of the room to the kitchen.

Outside was a humid, summery scene. The sunflowers had

been spoiled by the constant dampness, and since no one had gardened for some time, the weeds were thick and the rich black soil in the backyard was totally hidden under a lush green carpet. It was alarming and disheartening to see weeds prosper while the food crops were lying ruined. And, after all the unseasonable spring rain, the rainy season had followed giving an impression of endless dreariness. The faces of the farmers expressed the unhappy prospect of two consecutive years' poor harvest. Their rice crops had fared badly because the young plants had become waterlogged and had rotted before their roots were secure in the soil.

Curious as to the fate of the herb garden, Kae walked in the drizzle, hoping for a heavy downpour that would match the intensity of her emotions. The discord between Otsugi and herself preoccupied her thoughts and vexed her to the extent that she hardly thought about the dangerously high level of the Kinokawa River, which was likely to flood and already threatened the residents along its banks. Inspecting the herb bed seemed like a suitable activity for a doctor's wife. Besides, it relieved her to realize that she actually had a role and status in a family in which she was always under her in-laws.

Water was excellent for these herbs, which were really wild plants, and they were sprouting even more profusely than the weeds. Kae was amazed to find some flowers blooming and leaves branching off in all directions. The Korean Morning Glories, almost a transparent white in color, swam in a sea of green. How plentiful were these Crazy Eggplants! Poisonous, vigorous, multiplying rapidly as their seeds dispersed everywhere, of all the herbs in the garden these purple-stemmed ones were the hardiest. Their white flowers, so graceful and lovely from a distance, revealed strong, sharp-edged petals up close. Kae despised them since they never failed to remind her of the first time she saw Otsugi, and such recollections now provoked her anger. She wondered why she had been under the spell of Otsugi's charms, the same woman who was just betrayed by her homely wrinkles. It occurred to her that Otsugi's obsession with her appearance and her attempts to conceal the lines in her skin were indications of a dreadful tenacity, and, of course, immodesty and poor taste. Kae decided that she could no longer bear to watch the fifty-year-old woman look in the mirror so often. It was as if her own womanliness were being exposed. But even more annoying was that Otsugi's behavior appeared natural, devoid of any pretense or wantonness, so that in the end Kae's frustration was exacerbated because she could do nothing about it.

Kae stretched out her hands and snatched the cold, wet flowers. One after the other she picked them in defiance, as she was too upset merely to contemplate their rapaciousness and beauty.

"Do you know the name of that flower?" inquired a voice overhead.

Kae had been too engrossed to hear footsteps. Clutching the flowers, the frightened girl stiffened, looked up at her husband, and tried to concentrate on the question.

"Isn't it *mandarage**?" she responded with some hesitation.

"Oh, so you know it, eh?"

Having called them Crazy Eggplants as a child, Kae did not want to remember that it was her mother-in-law who had explained the medicinal qualities of these herbs to her. But the memory came in spite of herself, along with the realization that she had been gathering them without permission. Umpei noticed her embarrassment, knelt beside her, and also began to gather the *mandarage*.

* *mandarage* (*Datura alba* Nees)

65

"I can't wait until they've seeded in the fall."

Kae had no idea what he meant and couldn't decide what to do with the bunch in her hand.

"This is an excellent opportunity to experiment. Now, these petals must be dried before mildew sets in. Where would there be a shady place?"

"How about on the kitchen beams? It's quite dry up there."

"Good idea."

As Umpei picked another handful, Kae made a large pocket in her kimono by tucking her hanging sleeves in her sash, and into this her husband dropped the flowers without a word. The rain was less bothersome now. Kae was thrilled to be alone with her husband, away from everyone.

"I want you to wipe them with a dry cloth."

"I will."

"And be sure to throw it away afterwards."

"All right. Are the flowers poisonous?"

"Not as poisonous as *uzu*.* But be careful anyway."

"I will."

"Has Yonejiro returned yet?"

"No, I don't think so."

"Please let me know the moment he's back."

"All right."

Her heart was pounding throughout the conversation. It was the first time that they had spoken together in complete privacy during the daytime. Holding the *mandarage* firmly against her body, Kae raced back to her room. There she found her mother-in-law in the process of airing her kimonos, neatly spreading them over the matted floor.

"What's the matter?" asked Otsugi in an accusing tone, her eyes peering at the soaked girl and the flowers.

* *uzu* (*Tuber aconiti*)

66

"Umpei told me to dry them on the kitchen beams," replied Kae, more composed than usual. Otsugi's noticeable displeasure gave her a sense of superiority.

Kae took out one of her cotton kimonos from a drawer and tore it up without the slightest regret. What did it matter if she had to sacrifice one or two to help her husband? After all, he had asked her and not his mother to perform the task.

Meanwhile Otsugi seemed to be mumbling something that sounded to Kae like "How late Yonejiro is," implying that Kae would never have been asked to do the job had the assistant been at home. But the contented Kae simply continued to wipe the wet *mandarage*.

"Those flowers are poisonous. Never mix that cloth with others. Be sure to remember."

"Yes, Mother. Umpei told me to throw it away."

"And wash your hands thoroughly. It would be very dangerous to touch anything in the kitchen if you don't."

"Yes, Mother," said the girl cheerfully despite Otsugi's stern, commanding voice. She was just too happy to care.

Otsugi quickly finished what she was doing, glared once more at Kae, and left.

Having lost their former vigor, the funnel-shaped *mandarage* flowers now lay completely lifeless, as if their very spirit had been crushed. As she dried and placed them in a winnow one by one, her thoughts wandered back to that first night with her husband. She blushed, and sighed in relief that her mother-in-law had gone.

It had been so many days after Umpei's return! At that time it was customary for a samurai family to have separate quarters for husband and wife, but Otsugi could not ignore the marital situation indefinitely. One night, avoiding her daughter-in-law's eyes, she told Kae to go to Umpei's room. The young wife, burning with shame, then entered, holding her pillow against her bosom. In spite of the fact that they were man and wife, Kae found it painful to make this visit. Umpei's room, which by day was transformed into an examination area, was adjacent to her father-in-law's and separated only by a sliding partition. On the other side slept Yonejiro and Ryoan, giving Kae additional anxieties. What a difference it would have made had this been her wedding night, when she was still not familiar with the house. Indeed, it would have been proper for Otsugi to have given her own room over to the couple and to have spent the night with her daughters. But since she had no such intention, Kae was forced to go to her husband. How could she not suspect Otsugi of malice?

Umpei behaved quite naturally toward his trembling wife. But when his hand grabbed one of her breasts, Kae was shocked and had to suppress a cry as she squirmed out of his grasp.

"Did that hurt?" His voice rose far above a whisper.

But it was not the kind of question the surprised, timid girl could answer. So Umpei repeated his inquiry and continued to fondle her breasts, grasping them tightly or pulling at her nipples.

Kae had no knowledge of bedroom intimacies beyond what she had been told by Tami. And since she was quite uninformed about foreplay, she concluded that Umpei's actions were motivated by professional curiosity. She remembered the evening he said that the breast was a vital part of a woman's body and could not be operated on, even for cancer. Still, it appalled her to see him act like a doctor in these circumstances.

"Ouch!" This time she could not prevent a plaintive cry.

Umpei immediately let go and very gently began to caress her nipples with his palms. Kae wriggled at the unexpected sensation of pleasure until she forgot herself and everything around her, and surrendered her body to her husband.

The unending rain that night had been especially depressing, for the silence seemed to be contained within the walls of the house. By morning Kae feared that her cry of pain had been heard in the adjoining rooms, indeed that it had reverberated all the way to Otsugi's room and that it had probably not been associated with breast pain. Not that Kae was concerned with the thoughts of her weak and bedridden father-in-law! It was rather the reactions of Yonejiro, Ryoan, Okatsu, Koriku, and the smaller children that made her feel ashamed and more isolated than ever. It seemed as if everyone were behaving strangely toward her, even avoiding direct contact with her. Change was less obvious in her mother-in-law, who rarely spoke to her anyway.

After Naomichi's death, Umpei moved into his father's room. Kae then began to feel less anxious about the noises, and her husband in turn grew more daring. Sometimes, with the lamp still lit, he embraced her and stared at her body, his huge eyes barely blinking, as he fondled her breasts. Kae usually covered her mouth with her sleeve to prevent any sounds from escaping, and wished it would soon be over. But while her mind said one thing, her body wanted another. She enjoyed the strong sensations of pleasure and often moaned, noticing in the midst of everything that the mole on Umpei's neck appeared terribly large.

The most unpleasant part was returning to her own room, where Otsugi was usually asleep. There were nights, however, when Kae was so carried away that she slept at her husband's side until the first cock crowed, signalling it was time to hurry back to her bed. On these occasions she had to prepare herself for the scrutiny of the pale-faced woman who had already combed her hair, and for the disdain that was unspoken but that was almost audible nonetheless: "What was that cry?

Till dawn? What a woman!" But though the voice pierced her like a rusty nail, it strengthened her nerve.

Kae tied strings around the flat basket in which the dried flowers were neatly arranged. Then, springing lightly to her feet, she replaced her wet clothes with a red silk kimono which she took from a wide chest of drawers. Unlike the cotton striped one, it felt light and comfortable against her skin, matching her cheery mood. The short time she had spent with her husband picking *mandarage* had helped assuage her fears, so that she cared much less what either Otsugi or her sisters-in-law would think of her. An optimistic, happy Kae entered the kitchen and astonished the maid and Koriku with her gay attire.

"Help me, please." The wife of the head of the house spoke in a way that commanded respect. "I'm going to dry these flowers here," she said indicating a place on the ceiling where she thought the basket would be free of smoke and steam from the pots; then, standing on a stool held by the maid, she hung up the basket.

The joy which filled her whole being, in spite of the interminable rain, was reflected in the charming manner with which she greeted Yonejiro.

"Welcome home! You must be soaked. What have you there?" inquired Kae, noting something wriggling in his arms.

Yonejiro gently placed the three kittens, peeking out of his straw raincoat, on the floor. They were too timid to move.

"The people who gave them to me," he explained, "did not know what to do with a big litter when it's difficult enough these days to feed human beings. They were grateful to me for taking them. I wanted to rush back to show the doctor, but the family insisted on feeding me instead of providing cat food."

As he chatted, he lifted three more kittens from the fish

70

basket hanging around his waist without bothering to undo his raincoat. Kae counted to herself: now they had eleven kittens in all, including those in a cage on the veranda. Yonejiro also looked for stray dogs, and now they had nine tied up in the backyard. For reasons unknown to his wife, Umpei had begun to collect these animals shortly after his return from Kyoto. Kae was relieved that at least this batch would not eat as much as the dogs. She wondered for a while whether she should hand the mewing kittens over to Okatsu and Koriku, but then decided to care for them herself. "A wife ought to try to please her husband," she thought, "even if it means elbowing her in-laws aside."

A little later, a traveling pharmacist from a distant region dropped in on the Hanaokas. By then Ryoan had also returned. The household grew more lively, as everyone gathered to hear the guest discuss various aspects of the natural calamity which was entering its third year.

"It's a real disaster. In some places, people are dying one after another. Kishu seems better off, although this year certainly won't be as good as the last. Much of the rice kept in the storehouses in the castle has already been consumed." His speech was rapid, like a huckster on the street. "Not only have rice crops been destroyed, but this damnable rain has caused widespread epidemics and flooding. It seems that once you catch a cold, you never recover. But . . . these kind of problems are certainly to the pharmacists' profit. I'll give you an example. No matter how expensive ginseng becomes, everyone buys it. I guess nothing is more precious than survival. You know the price of rice is nearly twice as much as last year. I tell you, the situation is very serious. As far as medicines go, wholesalers will go on raising their rates, saying their stocks are finished. I personally think that pharmacists should be as

71

philanthropic as doctors. It goes against my conscience to raise prices unfairly. But I just don't have enough merchandise to supply everyone's needs, since almost every house has at least one sick member in it." While the vendor was sharing his tales of the misery and depression around Kyoto with Umpei and his assistants, he did not forget to make excuses for his own high prices.

"You see, Doctor, it isn't just food that's rotting. The body is decaying too. For example, there's a strange disease going around now near Sakai."

"What are you talking about?" Umpei's eyes sparkled and he leaned forward, keenly interested.

"They say that the bones decay and protrude. Certain areas, which can be anywhere on the body, become painful when pressed. The wife of one of my customers is suffering right below her eye. The whole thing is bulging. I'm sure it's catching. From what I hear, there are maybe ten such cases."

"Are they cysts?" asked Ryoan of Umpei.

"No. From the description they may be bone tumors. Their hardness is due to liquid in the bone marrow."

"Do you think the disease is infectious?"

"Probably not. I think these are cases of malnutrition caused by the long famine."

"Can they be cured?"

"Probably," replied Umpei in an offhand manner.

The vendor rubbed his hands, beat the drum that all such vendors carry, and paid the doctor a compliment: speaking in a mixture of the Kishu dialect and that of his own part of the country, he said that Umpei's special training in Kyoto must have made him an excellent doctor. Then he lifted the oil-cloth covering his basket and took out the medicines Umpei had ordered.

"We have *Tuber aconiti* and *Cnidium officinale*, which you asked for some time ago. You can have them at the old prices. But *Angelica acutilola* and *Angelica grabrae* are in great demand because they are used to stop bleeding. Really, it wasn't easy to fill your order. I want you to understand the situation. As for the prices . . . I leave them up to you."

The dogs began to bark all at once. When the startled merchant asked about the noise, Umpei explained that he was keeping about ten dogs in the house.

"And why do you have ten dogs?" asked the astonished man.

"We have more animals if you count the cats," replied Umpei.

"I know there are many stray dogs and cats around."

"If you bring me some, I'd be willing to pay you."

"Really? That's very kind of you."

"In order to save human life, I need dogs and cats," offered Umpei by way of explanation.

But the pharmacist was too surprised to ask any more questions. "You're absolutely right, Doctor." He nodded in somewhat irrelevant agreement and changed the subject.

"Well, depressing weather, isn't it? I would prefer the rain to stop rather than to have an increase in sales. I mean that sincerely. I've been told that this is the first time in history it has rained for two years, and there's no end in sight. For a traveling man like myself, being out in bad weather all the time can be fatal. I just can't afford the old proverb: 'The doctor is always the last person to take care of his own health.' So whenever I come to an inn, I make it a habit to prepare a drink that will keep me from catching cold."

"Fewer people can afford to pay for medicine nowadays, isn't that right?" asked Umpei.

"Oh, yes. When they can't afford rice and wheat to cook

porridge for the sick, how can they buy medicines? The people in Kishu, however, are still better off than elsewhere, perhaps because the Kishu lord has been generous in distributing money and food out of his own stores in the castle. In other places, the death toll from starvation has reached over one hundred thousand."

"Lord Harusada is indeed a compassionate ruler. I've heard that in southern Kishu the misery is much greater than here in the north."

Ryoan agreed with Umpei, and in turn recounted a story he had heard at the house of one of his patients. The merchant nodded and told of more unfortunate incidents he had witnessed on his travels. The longer the group listened to these catastrophes, the more depressed they became, for these dreadful tales touched everyone's heart.

"Please have some tea," urged Kae, entering with a tray. Still dressed in her bright red kimono, her appearance injected a dissonant note into the solemn atmosphere. Everyone was taken aback. But, despite Otsugi's critical eyes, she cheerfully served tea.

VIII

Kae had become pregnant two years later. According to the records, during those five unfortunate years in which disease and starvation ravaged the country, the number of deaths reached well over several hundred thousand. In Kishu province where the local government took good care of its people and where there weren't many deprived peasants to begin with, the situation stayed comparatively calm, without the peasant uprisings that occurred in other regions. Yet the Hanaokas were poorer than ever, so that Kae, Okatsu, Koriku, and even the smaller sisters were compelled to resume weaving. Their poverty was neither the consequence of the rise in prices, nor of too few patients. On the contrary, Umpei was so flooded with patients within one year of his return that he often remained in the examination room from early morning until late at night. In Nate, as elsewhere, the persistent rain caused all sorts of problems, including disease, and the dreaded outbreak of bone tumors, which was originally just in and around Sakai, had spread to those living along the upper reaches of the Kinokawa River.

But although patients were numerous, only a small portion of those who visited the doctor could pay for their treatment. Besides, Umpei, noted for his generosity, never stinted in dispensing medication nor in making ample concoctions and ointments out of expensive medicinal herbs. And still more patients flocked to him, from across the river and from as far away as Yamato. Those suffering from malnutrition were destitute. But some gave potatoes in lieu of payment, while others, hearing that Umpei liked cats and dogs, brought these animals to the house. Such expressions of gratitude by no means yielded a profit. And however zealously the women worked, their income hardly sufficed to pay for the costly medicines, much less feed the whole household. Of course, it was expected that the family of a doctor live frugally so that no one ever complained. And despite the hatred she bore Otsugi, Kae could never forget the proud manner in which her mother-in-law had prescribed the code of conduct for a doctor's wife.

They subsisted on millet porridge mixed with small diced potatoes. But upon discovering Kae's pregnancy, Otsugi cooked rice for her daughter-in-law and gave her all she could eat of it, along with extra portions of silver carp or smelt— nutritious, precious foods in those days of shortage, some of them occasionally contributed by Umpei's patients. Like most pregnant women, Kae was hungry all the time. But she was unwilling to eat, since it was as painful for her to go hungry as it was to feel obligated to Otsugi for special treatment. Her hesitation did not go unnoticed. One day, Otsugi lectured her rather formally.

"I think your reluctance is quite foolish. I understand that you might be uncomfortable eating in front of the others, but consider the one coming into this world. The baby belongs to the Hanaokas, and may be our future heir. So, it's your duty to produce a healthy child. Regard these foods as necessities for your baby's nourishment. Please, I urge you to eat them with all our blessings."

Whoever overheard her must have presumed Otsugi intended to remove her daughter-in-law's inhibitions at the dinner table. In fact, tears of gratitude were shed by Kae's mother herself when she learned of Otsugi's kindness toward her daughter. But since nowhere in that admirable speech could Kae find any consideration of her alone, she concluded that Otsugi's seeming thoughtfulness concealed a carefully calculated plan. Besides, if the newborn was to be a full-blooded Hanaoka, was she, Kae, the bearer of this child, to remain an outsider forever? Were her teeth, tongue, and stomach nothing but pestle and mortar, merely the instruments to feed the Hanaoka heir? She felt physically repelled by the food. In the first place, she sensed Otsugi's solicitude was a curse in disguise; in the second, she imagined that the Hanaokas would stuff her for nine months until the baby arrived, and then expect her to die; and lastly, she associated her fate with the numerous dogs and cats who had been buried under the persimmon tree.

Yet the foods were so superbly inviting that in spite of her apprehension and desire to resist, her healthy animal instincts prevailed, and she began to eat. And, as if she had relied on this happening, Otsugi used to place small amounts of fruits and nuts beside her loom. Although she would have enjoyed throwing all of it in Otsugi's face, Kae's hunger was insatiable, and she consumed everything in sight. Afterwards she felt miserable, like a stuffed squirrel, and she despised Otsugi even more than before.

In her seventh month of pregnancy, when her belly grew too large for her to bend forward over the loom, Kae had to stop weaving. She either sat or leaned against a wall post in her room, while she made vests and diapers out of her old clothes. She moved rather slowly now; but, of course, she had no reason to hurry.

"Kae!" Otsugi entered the room and chose to sit down a little behind her daughter-in law rather than beside her. Kae would have had to turn around to look at her, but guessing that Otsugi also preferred an indirect confrontation, Kae continued her sewing.

"Yes, Mother."

"Your confinement is approaching, isn't it?"

It was in fact two months away. But Kae could not figure out what Otsugi wanted, for her tone was coaxing, so she again answered softly in the affirmative.

"I want to discuss it with you. I believe it's customary in Nate for a woman to have her first baby in the home of her parents, although I don't know too much about this tradition because I came from across the river."

It was true. Kae recalled that her brother's wife had returned to her own home before the birth of their first child. But Kae was slow to reply.

"Is that so?" Had she said she too wanted to go home, her mother-in-law would have quickly consented, and might have even added that she had no wish to detain her. But since Kae did not answer in that way, Otsugi had to find an alternative.

"Please think it over. Umpei-san has already agreed that it's a good idea."

Kae knew that pregnant women often become irritable with very little provocation. However, at her mother-in-law's words, she felt the blood rushing to her head. Adding the honorific "san" to the eldest son's name was not peculiar in Kishu province where the family heir was accorded particular respect, but Otsugi's familiarity with Umpei had an intimate ring about it and infuriated Kae whenever she heard the suffix used. Besides, she was angry with Otsugi for obtaining Umpei's acquiescence without consulting her beforehand. It made her feel as though she were being driven out of the house. . . . And the affectation with which Otsugi alluded to the local custom! Kae was sure that it existed across the river in Chonomachi where Otsugi was born, as well as in Nate. And why did the couple have to separate at all? Wasn't Umpei delivered by Otsugi's husband in this house? How many times had Naomichi told that story! Why shouldn't the Hanaokas start a new tradition by having the first baby delivered by the husband? Kae scorned Otsugi's icy kindness. The idea of going home had been the farthest thing from her mind.

The Imoses, who knew nothing of their daughter's situation, rejoiced at Kae's return.

"I wanted to send you good foods, but I was afraid of offending the Hanaokas. Now that I see you weren't deprived, I'm truly relieved," said her mother.

"Cook something tasty for Kae. Get some carp from the pond. And make rice cakes too. Let her eat to her heart's content," added Sajihei, as he began to fuss over his daughter.

"Kae, I want you to eat as much as you can so that you'll give birth to a healthy baby."

Sajihei had worried a great deal about the Hanaokas since even his prosperous family had been affected by the years of scarcity. Having ceased collecting food from his tenant farmers (who gave it him as rent), he seldom had any to spare for his villagers. Consequently, when he and his wife discovered that

Otsugi had given Kae all she could eat, they gushed with gratitude, and Sajihei himself showered her with praise.

"There is a proverb that says, 'Even second-best is too good for a daughter-in-law.' It's so common to hear of a mother-in-law tormenting the wife of her son. We must really be thankful. No mother-in-law has ever been as kind to her daughter-in-law."

"I agree. Otsugi's reputation is completely justified. Kae is a lucky girl. Now I know we chose the right family for her. And Umpei is gaining more and more prestige, just as predicted." The gratified mother seemed to be taking the credit.

Exasperated with the direction of the conversation and unable to control her rancor, Kae burst into a fitful sobbing that caused her whole body to contort. Her mother was naturally surprised, but she embraced and consoled her, thinking it was only the fatigue and anxieties of pregnancy that Kae was expressing now that she was at her mother's side.

"There's nothing to get upset about, dear. Come on, cheer up! Your troubles will be over as soon as the baby is born. You must rest a lot and take it easy. Look only at beautiful objects and think about happy things, Kae. They say that the fear is greater than the danger, so it will be easier delivering the baby than worrying about it. Please, Kae, you've got to look after yourself—physically and mentally. Please calm down."

Mentally? Kae could hold her tongue no longer and began to blurt out everything that had been rankling in her heart over the years. She started with Otsugi's hideous wrinkles under her cosmetics, and then condemned her lack of wisdom, her coldness, and the dreadful manner in which she neglected the appearance of her son and daughters. It was Kae's contention that Otsugi preferred them dowdy and uncomely so that by contrast she always seemed attractive. As proof, Kae pointed out that her mother-in-law stared at her critically whenever she changed into a pretty kimono. Finally, Kae declared that she had been wanted by the clever, calculating woman during Umpei's absence only to weave so that the Hanaoka income would be increased; but the moment she was unable to sit at the loom, she was ordered back to her own family.

Her mother was bewildered at first, stunned in fact by the acrimony with which Kae poured out her grievances. Embarrassed by the unexpected turn of events, she sat in silence and reviewed each complaint. Otsugi's ugly, wrinkled face! That was indeed unreasonable. In the eyes of others, Otsugi was still as beautiful as ever. And what credibility could be given to the charge that Otsugi deliberately permitted her family to dress shabbily so that her own beauty would be magnified? People would surely laugh at such an outrageous idea, she concluded. As for Kae's suspicions about the money she earned when she arrived there as a bride—at that, Kae's mother began to doubt her daughter's sanity.

Her mother frowned, but her voice was soft as she scolded her daughter. "If you keep talking about your perfect mother-in-law in that way, you'll be punished for your ingratitude."

Kae let out an almost animal-like cry. In her extreme vexation she was losing all restraint.

"What's the matter with you? What will you do if all of this affects the baby? Now stop it, Kae, please."

Remembering her own pregnancies and how easily she became enraged in those days, she tried to be more compassionate and soothing.

Kae realized that she had not revealed other aspects of the conflict. For example, she had not mentioned that she was jealous of Otsugi for having borne Umpei and shared some thirty years of life with him. Nor could she have explained why she sensed that Otsugi's relationship with her son was more romantic than motherly, or how strange it had been the first night, when Otsugi had urged Umpei to sleep alone. Because it was not possible for her to make these disclosures, Kae felt that her mother's picture of her situation at the Hanaokas was terribly inaccurate and distorted. Certainly she knew that her mother would have been altogether confused had she been told that Otsugi wanted to prevent Umpei himself from delivering the baby.

After a short pause, her mother continued. "I, too, had problems with my mother-in-law. But since she had given life to my dear husband, I used to tell myself to tolerate her. But, Kae, you must believe me. There is no comparison between my mother-in-law and Otsugi. Mine used to find fault with practically everything I did. Really, I used to wonder why she hated me so much. If I stayed in bed because of morning sickness, she would accuse me of being lazy. Several times a day I had to clean the toilet so that I might have a beautiful baby. Eventually my kimono absorbed the horrid smells of the toilet bowl, and since my nose was overly sensitive during pregnancy, my head ached all day long. Yet I still had to crawl around the toilet with a washcloth." She grumbled at the recollection of her youth in the Imose household. Kae seemed calmer.

"But, you see," continued her mother, "when my daughter-in-law became pregnant, I prayed that God give us a healthy child. Whenever I went to the family shrine and lit a candle at Buddha's altar, I asked Him to grant us a robust, clever grandchild. Then, when it came to your pregnancy, my wishes changed. I prayed for your good health, an easy delivery, and speedy recovery from your confinement. It was *your* welfare I prayed for, and not that of the unborn child's. These were my true feelings. Just now, while I was listening to your story, the thought struck me that I must have caused that poor young daughter-in-law of mine similar tribulations—naturally without knowing what I was doing, and the idea made me sweat. Look at my palms!"

These hours with her mother turned out to be the most precious of Kae's visit. She mulled over their conversations very often before her confinement, hoping to find the peace of mind that was essential for a mother and her future baby. But when she happened to recall the garden scene, that day when she and Otsugi picked the blooming *mandarage* together and had said to each other that they had been fated to become mother and daughter, Kae could neither forgive Otsugi nor dissipate her anxieties.

"By the way," said her mother, trying to divert her attention, "I've heard Umpei has a fine new student."

"That's right. He comes from Hashimoto on Mt. Koya, someone by the name of Nakagawa Shutei. I was told he's quite capable even though he's very young. He, too, studied in Kyoto for several years."

"And I've heard that Umpei is becoming famous. He's a respected teacher now."

"Oh, yes. Nakagawa and other students refer to him as the respected Dr. Seishu."

"Well, well! The respected Dr. Seishu indeed! . . . Then you must be the 'respected doctor's wife.' "

"Oh, no. We're not that famous. Besides, my mother-in-law supervises everything. I hardly have any role there."

The conversation inevitably returned to Kae's grudge. But Kae's mother, who was the lady of the most important family in Nate, had little time to spend with her daughter alone. Until these years of famine, starvation, and misery, she had been

83

accustomed to a serene, rather uneventful life at home. But nowadays she shared her husband's responsibilities and attended to some of the problems of the villagers; she did her best to alleviate the plight of women, especially pregnant women, by caring for them and making sure they were given enough to eat. It was her belief, almost a religious conviction, that unless every pregnant woman succeeded in bearing a child that year, her own daughter's life was in jeopardy.

The ever-recurring antagonism toward Otsugi might have been Kae's unconscious way of distracting herself from what really bothered her—something which she dared not reveal to anyone, not even her mother. A tacit agreement existed among the Hanaokas never to divulge family secrets. Now, coinciding with the deaths of countless numbers of dogs and cats over the past two years was the departure of Shimomura Ryoan, who had decided to start his own medical practice at Myoji temple across the river. His leaving was natural after the death of Naomichi, his teacher, to whom he had been exceedingly devoted. But Kae suspected that he left because of Umpei's strange practices, and Yonejiro also seemed to think so.

In the bedroom of Umpei, now called Dr. Seishu, there were always a few animals asleep. Each had been given a bowl of rice porridge cooked in fish stock and some drug, whose ingredients were mixed by the doctor himself. Within a short time they reacted queerly, making all sorts of abnormal sounds: one groaned and lay down flat on his belly; another yelped frantically and circled round and round the same spot; a cat mewed sadly, stretching its claws spasmodically. Whenever a dog wandered out of the compound, it was Yonejiro's job to run after it. Eventually, however, after these first reactions, all of them went to sleep.

In the beginning, these animals with different names were

fed by Yonejiro and Shutei. Kae had taken over the task when the two assistants seemed overburdened with work. In accordance with Dr. Seishu's extravagant demands, the animals received the very best foods while the human members of the house remained undernourished. Only the animals and the pregnant Kae had really consumed enough, which explains Kae's unavoidable association of herself with them.

One day, quite by chance, Kae witnessed the following sight as she was going to feed the animals. There was a cat named Miru. Holding it by the neck, Seishu was pushing its face over and over into a bowl filled with liquor until the unfortunate animal became wild, mewed frantically, and started to choke from the strong alcohol. The cat was absolutely drunk before Seishu noticed his wife, staring in utter stupefaction, standing nearby.

"You know, this is the effect of *mandarage*," he said smilingly.

Kae didn't know what he was talking about. But she could distinguish the smell of liquor because her sensitivity to smell was heightened by her pregnancy.

"Remember the flowers we picked? I mixed their juice with alcohol and gave it to the cat. Come and observe the results in half an hour."

"All right."

Kae hurried out of the room. But her curiosity overcame her fears and she returned. She thought the cat would have gone mad after eating Crazy Eggplant. Beyond that, she had no idea whatsoever of what her husband was trying to accomplish. When she timidly peeped in, Seishu was recording minute details of the experiment in his thick notebook. Noticing his wife, he glanced up.

"It's time, is it?" Then he sat down near the cat who was

asleep in a corner of the room and took its pulse under one leg.

Kae watched while he stuck a probe into Miru's side causing convulsions, and blood gushed out after its extraction. His face expressionless, Seishu then continued to observe the cat, indifferent to anyone else, including his shivering wife. When she felt wobbly, as though she might faint, Kae tiptoed out of the room. Miru never got up from the bloodstained corner, and four days later was buried under the persimmon tree.

Alongside Miru in the room had been a spotted dog called Kumomaru and a ginger one named Uzuichi. Both had been forcefed with food and drugs and slept with legs outstretched.

Was it Kae's condition alone that aggravated her highly emotional nature? Perhaps. In any case, she had constant nightmares. On many a night she awakened to find Otsugi trying to comfort her.

"Here, Kae, have a drink. You were screaming again."

But in that lovely face, Kae saw only the continuation of those bad dreams. Even after she returned to her parents, she was still haunted by the animals. How she longed now for old Tami, who had given her so much self-confidence and security! She would have been able to confide in her, even those things she dared not tell her mother. Tami would have listened and taken her part unconditionally, without judging the rightness or wrongness of her confidences. And it would have relieved her troubled mind to describe the terrible deaths of the animals. It was understandable under the circumstances for Kae to feel saddened by the loss of her nursemaid friend, who was virtually her foster mother.

Restless and afraid that her newborn might be cursed by evil spirits emanating from the dead dogs and cats unless she unburdened her heart, she decided to visit Tami's grave in her last month of pregnancy. Her mother agreed to the trip and assigned an elderly maid as an escort, reminding both her and Kae repeatedly to take precautions against falling. With motherly concern, she seems to have permitted whatever was required to mitigate her daughter's awful temper.

Tami had been laid to rest in a cemetery which was located at the foot of Mt. Katsuragi. After a fifteen-minute walk, the women reached the site of a small gravestone, whereupon Kae instructed her companion to go back a little. In an absent-minded way, she then knelt down and prayed in front of the old tombstone belonging to this tenant farmer family who had been in the Imoses' service for several generations. In the midst of her prayers, Kae felt that everything she had wanted to express had already reached Tami's ears. And, as she looked at the weather-beaten stone that was difficult to read, her mood became philosophical; and she began to ask herself if this were the final destination for all humanity.

After a while, holding her bulging belly, she managed to get to her feet. Nothing had actually been said aloud, but Tami had apparently succeeded in freeing her mind because labor pains began as soon as they started down the mountainous path. Having borne children herself, the old woman knew exactly what to do. When the pain temporarily ceased, she made Kae walk, and when it resumed, she rubbed Kae's back and tried to reassure her that this first birth would take at least half a day. It took them twice as long to make the return trip.

Once home, Kae's mother ordered the maids to boil water, and Kae to wash her hair in preparation for her lengthy confinement in bed. The pain, which became excruciating at times, surprised Kae by its unusual force and then by its sudden disappearance. Her body was wracked with groans, which she could not suppress, and crawling on the floor, she scratched at the tatami in agony. Soon she bled, soaking her underwear and bed. Her thoughts wandered to the dog, Uzuichi, recalling how he had groaned and vomited blood, and his companion, Kumomaru, who had suddenly stiffened his legs in agony before he died. Kae was terrified. A clammy sweat covered her forehead, and in her bottomless fear she screamed for Tami over and over. At the peak of her suffering, when she imagined her pelvis would crack and her body would come apart, she felt something warm slip through the birth canal. The pain subsided. Like a fish splashing in water, the baby jumped out, its cry piercing the air.

Kae never dreamed of the joys that followed. The intense pain, which lasted nearly half a day, had penetrated her entire body and had threatened to tear her in two. But the very moment the baby emerged, it all vanished, and she was left with the realization that she had produced a child. In retrospect, the physical anguish seemed like thunder and lightning rolling through the darkness. And for the first time, she had reason to believe Naomichi's story of Seishu's birth.

The immediate pleasures of motherhood may be compared to those of a conqueror during his first moments of triumph. Kae decided that from then on, no Hanaoka would be able to intimidate her since none of them could bear Seishu's child.

The news of the birth brought Seishu rushing to his wife's side. Staring at the sleeping child in the crib, he commented happily, "What a beautiful baby! How about calling her Koben? You know, I expected a girl."

Of course, wishful parents sometimes call their children good-looking, but in this case Kae had to admit that Koben bore a certain resemblance to Otsugi and that she was likely to become a beauty. After years of detesting her mother-in-law and bearing her grudges, it felt strange to think of her as beautiful once more. The change was welcome. It had not occurred to

Kae that her present sense of complacency stemmed from the delights of victory.

Three days later Otsugi came to the Imoses for a short visit.

"Thank you for your hard work, Kae. Please give us a little boy next time, won't you?"

It was as if an icicle had suddenly touched her warm body. The superiority and pride of a woman who had borne a male child were all revealed in the greeting. Kae was crushed. Her voice, barely audible, was full of bitterness.

"Yes, next time."

"Well, Kae, take care of yourself, and come back after a good rest. Don't worry about the housework. There are enough women around."

She turned to Kae's parents and bade them farewell with her perfect smile. "Please look after her. She is our very dear daughter-in-law."

IX

During the summer of Koben's fourth year, it was apparent that Okatsu was ill. Kae was the first to observe that her sister-in-law now carried the water bucket in her left hand, favoring her right shoulder, and that she walked awkwardly. Shortly thereafter, the quiet, hard-working woman began to complain of fatigue at the loom and had to stop weaving. Now that the famine had passed and Seishu's fame had spread throughout the area resulting in a busy practice and reasonably good income, the Hanaoka women no longer worked to provide for the family. Whatever they earned was used for their personal needs.

"Is something wrong, Sister?" inquired Kae, unwilling to let her observations go without comment.

"Does there seem to be?" smiled the embarrassed Okatsu, leaving the question unanswered.

She was thirty and unmarried. In those years when she might

have found a husband, she labored at the loom and contributed every cent to her brother's education, money which otherwise would have been set aside for her wedding day. Nor did her luck change after her brother's return. Five years of scarcity ensued, during which time no family could afford anything but burial costs. Naturally, she had not received any proposals. And if she had, Okatsu would have found it difficult to accept, since all of the Hanaoka women were needed to earn money for Seishu's expensive medicines. Still, if Okatsu had insisted on marrying, she probably could have done so, but without clothing or dowry. Her youth, like that of Koriku, her twenty-eight-year-old sister, had been devoted to her brother's career. As Otsugi had remarked after Koben's birth, there were indeed plenty of women around the house.

Okatsu's poor appetite and increasingly sallow complexion did not escape her mother's notice. But even with Otsugi, Okatsu declined to discuss her condition.

"If something is wrong, you should let your brother make a potion for you. His medicine always works. Otherwise, why would so many people come here from across the river and far-away Senshu province? The sooner you get treated the better," insisted her mother repeatedly.

Okatsu nodded, but showed no inclination to consult her brother.

One afternoon, the younger child, Tane, rushed into the room and reported in a screeching voice: "Elder Sister's breast is like a watermelon!"

Otsugi turned white. Yonejiro and Shutei gulped in amazement. All eyes shifted to Seishu, including those of Yogen, Shuzo, and Shosai, students who had recently joined him.

"Okatsu, let me see it," ordered Seishu with a grave, pained expression.

Resigned, Okatsu lay down on the examination mat. Koriku took her younger sisters out of the room, but Otsugi held Ryoan by the arm and sat behind Seishu, for she certainly expected her youngest son, now thirteen years of age, to become a doctor as well. Kae stood behind the students and watched.

Okatsu's breast was so greatly enlarged that Seishu's palm covered only a small part of the tender area.

"Does it hurt?" he asked his sister. The memory of the phrase and the manner in which he posed the question startled Kae.

"Yes."

"How long has it been like this?"

"Since the Peach Blossom Festival in March when I noticed a small lump."

"Why didn't you tell me then?"

Instead of replying, Okatsu calmly asked, "It's breast cancer, isn't it, Brother?"

Everyone in the room seemed paler than Okatsu at that moment. Seishu didn't answer. And Okatsu didn't repeat her question. Since the night of his return when breast cancer had been a topic of discussion, no effective treatment had been discovered for cases of malignant breast tumors. Aware of this fact, Okatsu knew that had she confided in her brother earlier, she still could not have been cured. The innocent woman whose virgin breast had never been caressed or given the chance to nurse a baby of her own was terminally ill.

"How could this happen to her!" wondered Kae, full of sadness.

Okatsu was treated with compresses, ointment, and a drink that helped reduce the inflammation. It was obvious to everyone that these measures served only to diminish the feeling of hopelessness. Okatsu knew it too. As her condition deteriorated and the pain grew more intense, the courageous woman asked for something to lessen her suffering. Some time after the years of famine, Seishu had developed an ointment which was an excellent local anesthetic and was used in operations to remove bone tumors. Patients who had survived his operations spoke highly of this painkiller. But in Okatsu's case, an operation was unthinkable; and unless the malignant area could be exposed, the ointment was useless. Yet, in her terrible agony, Okatsu begged to be allowed to swallow it for relief.

Seishu looked her straight in the eyes. "That medicine contains too much *uzu* and *mandarage* to drink," he said quietly. "Be brave and bear what you must."

"Then please give me something to let me die in my sleep," pleaded his sister. She was probably referring to the medication that had been given to the animals buried under the persimmon tree.

Otsugi left the room. The conversation was too painful. Tears streamed down Kae's cheeks. Otsugi, however, having regained her composure returned almost immediately to talk to her daughter.

"A doctor's obligation is to save lives. And he isn't permitted to put a patient to sleep, even if the pain is unbearable."

"Please operate on me then, Brother. I know you're good at it."

"If that were possible, do you think I'd leave you like this?"

"Then cut into my breast. If I should die, I would still feel satisfied knowing that I might have been helpful to you."

Otsugi let out an anguished moan at the thought of her daughter's death. Kae saw that her husband was crying silently, without tears, and that his black mole was quivering on his throat.

It was toward the end of the year that Otsugi dared to bring up the subject again. No one was in the mood to prepare for the New Year celebrations while a member of their family lay in misery near death.

"Since Okatsu insists, won't you try to use the painkiller on a compress?"

"It won't work for breast tumors," answered the doctor.

"But just to ease her mind."

"Do you want to kill Okatsu?" His sharp tone threw Otsugi off her guard.

"How dare you say that? Who would want to kill one's own daughter? If I could, I would take her place."

"Any medicine on a compress will go right into her mouth. Don't you understand, Mother, why she asked for it?"

The face of his bewildered mother expressed only fear. Thinking that too much had been said, Seishu began to speak more calmly, confiding what had long been bothering him.

"Breast cancer is considered fatal in women. However, it's not accurate to state that no cure has been recorded. While I was in Kyoto, I read in Nagatomi Dokushoan's *Journal* about a story he had heard concerning a Dutch physician, Van Tanno. These are his notes which I copied." Seishu took a thick notebook off his bookshelf, opened it at a bookmark and showed some Chinese script to his mother.

We have believed for many centuries that breast cancer is incurable. But, in a Dutch medical book, there are records of women who have been cured. In the early stages, an incision was made to remove the small, malignant portion, after which the breast was sewn back together. The disease was contained. While I understand and appreciate the possibilities of that fantastic operation, I haven't been able to try it myself. This precious document shall serve future generations.

95

"You see, Mother, ever since Okatsu became ill, I have been staring at this paragraph night and day. Her tumor is almost as large as my fist. And two more have developed, under her arm and on her shoulder. The malignancy is spreading, causing her condition to deteriorate so that she couldn't possibly sustain the pain and bleeding of an operation. If new anesthetics were available though, the whole picture could be different."

"I thought you had made up some kind of anesthetic now that your dogs and cats are all awake and walking around, and seldom die."

"Animals react differently from people. My experiments have never been made on humans, and I haven't a human subject. I know it's hard for you to lose your own daughter. But it is ten times harder for me as a doctor to watch my patient die than it is for me as a brother to have my sister pass away. I am frustrated by my limitations. I'm no match for Hua Tu. Understand the situation, please, Mother."

An outburst from the backyard interrupted them.

"Brother, Brother," called the younger girls.

"What's the matter?" As Seishu stood up, Yonejiro rushed in with the white cat, Byakusen.

"Doctor, look . . ."

"What happened?"

"He fell from the veranda and his head hit the stone step. Look at him."

Byakusen lay in front of Seishu, bleeding from the eyes, nose, and mouth, his legs slightly convulsed. Soon he was motionless.

"Did he fall by himself?"

"Yes. As he was going along the edge of the veranda, he tilted to one side and fell headlong."

About ten days earlier, Seishu had tested an anesthetic on

Byakusen. The animal had slept for three days and nights, insensitive even to a probe penetrating his side. His pulse, however, had continued to beat regularly. After he awoke he was given some salty, warm water. He then started to walk, haltingly—as if intoxicated. Yet, when his favorite food of rice porridge cooked in fish stock was placed in front of him, his appetite seemed normal. Nevertheless, he didn't bother to chase a mouse that ran right in front of him, so the poisonous drug had probably damaged his brain. Cats are very agile and generally land safely on their feet, even when thrown into the air, because of their flexible bodies and remarkable co-ordination. Yet this poor creature had slipped from the edge of the veranda and died almost instantly.

Kae also came to see what had happened. The sight of Bya-kusen's body left everyone speechless. Not because of the death itself; they were quite used to that. It was rather the way in which the creature had fallen so helplessly off a low veranda to his death that terrified them.

Okatsu died just after the beginning of the New Year. At the family gathering on New Year's Day, there was little to cele-brate. The youngest, Ryohei, didn't even request his usual second helping of rice cakes. Death was on everyone's mind. Actually, the Hanaokas had been in mourning long before Okatsu passed away.

Ryohei had observed the progression of his sister's cancer until the end. Was it her death itself, or the fact that she died so young that perplexed the boy, causing him to leave his grieving family and run off into the neighboring fields? On one such occasion, after he came back, he reported some of the gossip he had heard in the village.

"They're saying that Elder Sister died because of a curse by the dead cats and dogs."

"Be quiet. Don't you ever repeat that again," scolded Otsugi, whose face almost matched the pale blue of a nearby porcelain jar.

The Hanaokas had never neglected to perform a memorial service for each animal under the tree. Nowadays, however, those treated with the drug woke up after its affects wore off and stalked zombi-like about the house, their brains affected in the same way as Byakusen's. Perhaps the spirits of the dead could be appeased. But what could be done for these spiritless, lethargic animals? The curse which had brought about Okatsu's unfortunate death must be from these half-dead animals; at least, almost everyone in the Hanaoka house was inclined to think so. But Kae felt that such a belief, if it was held within the family, would disturb Seishu. She tried therefore to dispel these notions when she took it upon herself to calm her young brother-in-law.

"Don't think of Sister's death as a curse. If it were, Koben would surely never have been born. See, she's growing up to be a normal, healthy child."

Scarcely had the words left her lips, when Kae was struck by their implication. But it was too late. Sparks of anger flashed over Otsugi's face. It was obvious that in her frenzied grief, this poor mother must have believed that the curse had haunted her own daughter, yet eluded her daughter-in-law's child. Otsugi didn't say a word. Kae thought her silence was a result of her realization that such an interpretation was illogical.

The relationship between the women grew even colder after Okatsu's death. Having experienced the emotions of motherhood through Koben, Kae thought she understood Otsugi's suffering at the loss of her child. It had been Kae's hope to bury the bitterness, jealousy, and animosity she felt toward her mother-in-law and to comfort her in her time of sorrow. But

98

in contrast to Kae's mellowing, all of Otsugi's hostility, grief, and resentment for her loss were directed toward her daughter-in-law. During the funeral ceremonies, the two women never spoke to each other. And afterwards communication between them was carried on through Koriku, who was thirty by then and beyond the marrying age.

Shimomura Ryoan, who had been paying regular visits to the doctor's family after he left for Myoji temple, came to Okatsu's wake dressed in mourning clothes. He helped the distracted, heartbroken Hanaokas arrange the funeral. Seishu was exceedingly despondent. He appeared thin, as if he had suffered from a prolonged illness, and looked older than thirty-three. Looking at him, Ryoan saw the image of the aging Naomichi in his declining years. When the wake was over and the guests had gone, he tried to console Seishu, still sitting in front of his sister's coffin.

"I know it's hard to take. But if your disappointment affects your health, there will be a still sadder story here. You have to regard this as a natural event."

Seishu opened his large eyes and bellowed. "Do you mean that a doctor should believe in the ways of the natural world like a Buddhist monk? As long as disease, no matter what kind, causes death, it will be because medicine is imperfect. *I* killed Okatsu. *I* let her die. My skill as doctor is not enough. Don't you understand my agony?"

His shouting shook the cover of the coffin. Ryoan wasn't the only one frightened. Most of the students couldn't bear to watch their teacher in this rage, and left the room. Nakagawa Shutei, who was known to have said behind his teacher's back that a doctor should experiment surgically in the interests of medicine if the patient is doomed, said nothing. He may have reconsidered and realized that a doctor must undertake an operation only when he is confident that surgery will prolong his patient's life.

X

One beautiful spring day, the birds were chirping peacefully and the water splashed merrily as Kae washed clothes by the well. The famine was now only a memory. Even the problems of the previous Kishu lord, Harusada Kagenin, belonged to history. It was rumored that the former ruler had spent much of his clan's money to help the impoverished and suffering inhabitants in his domain, and as a consequence, his clan's annual stipend had been halved for more than six years. But that, too, was all over, and Kagenin's successor, Harutomi, was already in the tenth year of his reign. Kae remembered the late Kagenin because he had often stayed at the Imose house, the Kishu lord's quarters in Nate, and she herself had sometimes served him dinner. Of the present lord she knew nothing at all, except from hearsay about his extravagance at the castle.

Since people have a tendency to imitate those in higher positions, the villagers of Nate were spending more freely. Besides, several years of fruitful harvests after the famine had made new lifestyles possible. The frugal Hanaokas were not unaffected by the current trends.

Koriku had given up all hope of a family of her own, but the two youngest girls were of marriageable age. Although their finances were much improved compared to past years, the Hanaokas still had to economize to pay for the sumptuous weddings which occurred almost simultaneously. Thinking of the misfortunes of her elder daughters, Otsugi tried to insure a better fate for her younger ones, so she consented quickly to the two offers she received. Because of Seishu's excellent reputation, his sisters married into prestigious families, one of which lived in the distant town of Kuroye in Umiguchi province.

Only five Hanaokas remained. The second son, Jihei, opened a store of his own in Chonomachi after he completed his apprenticeship there with a merchant. The third son, who was trained for the priesthood, had a promising future as the head of the Shochiin temple on Mt. Koya. And the youngest, Ryohei, had now been in Kyoto for four years studying medicine. The Hanaokas suffered no hardships on his account.

But the actual number of people in the house was larger than before. More students had come to live, many of whom paid tuition. A small dormitory was constructed, and a maid was hired to look after their meals and laundry. With the increasing prosperity, Kae could have led the leisurely life of a great lady, fussing over herself like her mother-in-law. But she was too active to stay indoors and preferred to go out into the bright sunshine. Doing the laundry was by far her favorite form of relaxation. It was a wonderful sensation to feel the fresh water trickling through her fingers; besides, scrubbing her husband's clothes seemed to help her forget her mother-in-law's nastiness.

Kae had been with the Hanaokas for nearly fifteen years, certainly long enough to have established secure roots. Otsugi's frowns and smiles no longer affected her, and she knew how to avoid her whenever she sensed something unpleasant was about to happen. There were times when Kae's mood was even philosophical, and she told herself that discord was natural with any mother-in-law, in fact, that it was the usual state of affairs in every household although it wasn't discussed or even hinted at. If Kae observed a mother and her daughter-in-law getting on reasonably well, it seemed to her that they were deceiving each other in some clever fashion. But such was not the case at the Hanaokas. In this household, the two contrasting personalities of the extremely clever Otsugi and her daughter-in-law who lacked the quick wits to outmaneuver her collided constantly and often became mired in the entanglement. At the least, they had grown accustomed to a relationship of continual confrontation.

While Kae was rinsing the clothes and pouring out the dirty water from the basin, Koben ran over to her.

"Mother, come and see! Father's playing with a cat. It's fun!" And with this announcement, the child rushed back to the yard.

All the students were shouting excitedly. "Playing with a cat?" wondered Kae as she dried her hands and headed in the direction of the commotion. Seishu was in the middle of the group, laughing and holding a cat in his arms. Kae had not seen him so happy since before Okatsu's death.

Beaming joyfully, Yonejiro approached Kae. "You see, Mafutsu spins perfectly in the air."

Then Seishu noticed his wife and called out, "Watch. There

103

he goes." The cat who was thrown high in the air wriggled, mewed, but alighted safely. Not an especially spectacular performance for a cat. But Mafutsu had been lying in a corner for three days in a drugged sleep, not unlike Byakusen, who years ago had slipped to his death from the low veranda. Kae was deeply moved, for she realized that this was evidence that Seishu's continuous experimentation in anesthetics, going on for over ten years now, was nearing completion.

When Otsugi and Koriku came out of the house, Seishu again demonstrated, tossing the cat high in the air.

"Mafutsu is the right name for this one—the 'Narcotic One.' Did you know that Hua Tu performed numerous operations using *mafutsu* water?" he asked his mother.

"It looks like a great success. Congratulations! Your father would have been so pleased if he were here today," replied Otsugi in a trembling voice.

"Not really. This is just a cat, so it's not what I would call a huge success. There's a big difference between cats and people. Had I given a similar dosage to a person, I don't think it would have worked. I really don't know what amount is required to put someone to sleep and yet avoid possible poisonous side-effects. That's the question I face from now on." A shadow crossed his face as he spoke, probably because he was wondering how he could experiment on a human subject.

The wise mother read her son's thoughts, then stared at her radiant daughter-in-law, frowned, and without a word entered the house.

Her sudden displeasure in the midst of the small celebration was incomprehensible to Kae. Although she had learned not to question Otsugi's behavior, her reaction under these circumstances troubled her. "Why shouldn't she be happy?" Kae asked herself.

The riddle was soon solved. One night, while Kae was help-ing Seishu undress in his bedroom, the door opened and Otsugi entered, scarcely making a sound. The hour was late, and an intimacy between the couple was taking form. Feeling em-barrassed as if she were being exposed, Kae stood frozen. But Otsugi ignored her, sat in front of Seishu and began to talk to him in her inimitable, decisive manner.

"Umpei, please listen to me. What I have to say comes after many hours of reflection."

"What is it, Mother?"

"Today I visited your father's grave and confided my thoughts to him. I felt I heard him say that he would do the same if he were alive."

"What are you talking about?"

"Let me be the subject of your anesthetic experiment."

Kae drew in her breath sharply and eyed first Otsugi and then her husband. In an instant Seishu laughed, indicating that he rejected the whole idea.

"You're amazing, Mother. What a suggestion, and in the middle of the night! Don't worry about it. Please, I beg you, Mother, put it out of your mind and go to bed."

"No," she replied firmly. "Everyone close to you, Um-pei . . . except a fool, can see that your research would be complete if only you could test the drug on a person. I am the mother who gave birth to you, so I, more than anybody else, understand what you want to accomplish."

The words stung. ". . . Except a fool . . . ": the allusion could only be to Kae herself. "I am the mother who gave birth to you, so I, more than anybody else, understand . . . " It seemed another example of Otsugi's intention to assert her superior position with Seishu.

"Oh no! I decided long ago to offer myself. Please try it on me!" Kae's pronouncement was of course unexpected, probably because of its spontaneity.

"That is indeed absurd!" retorted Otsugi icily. "If something should happen to my dear daughter-in-law, how could I face the world? . . . No, don't feel obligated on my account. . . . And don't interfere. Just take care of yourself and watch the family thrive."

"You can't mean that! It's I, your daughter-in-law, who would not be able to face the world if I permitted you to take the medicine. How could I be happy afterwards? No, I will assume the responsibility no matter what."

"Absolutely not. I haven't much longer to live. I have outlived my husband. And I have no regrets. When Okatsu died I really wished to go with her since life can hold no further pleasure for me. All my children have grown up. Umpei has a splendid wife. Now I prefer to join my husband in the grave rather than continue in this house which is run by a younger generation. If my body could be of some use to my son, I would be more than grateful. You still have the important task of producing an heir for this family. Until then your body must be well cared for."

To anyone unfamiliar with their rivalry, the dialogue might have sounded noble. But Otsugi's clever tongue did not fool Kae. How ironic to have been called "dear daughter-in-law." The need to "produce an heir" was yet another reminder that Kae had only borne a girl. And there were no signs of a second pregnancy after ten years. Aware that this was her weak spot, Otsugi must have mentioned it deliberately, concluded Kae, who was beginning to feel desperate.

"They say that a childless woman, or one who hasn't borne a male after three years, should leave. I am such a useless woman—only one girl. Why do I deserve to live? I insist on being the subject. How can I let an older woman go through such an ordeal?"

Under the guise of self-debasement, Kae had daringly called her an old woman, a calculated challenge to Otsugi's pride in her youthful looks.

"Indeed, I am an old and useless woman; yet, after bearing eight children, I have a healthy body. Surely I can endure the experiment."

"I won't let you. It goes against my conscience as your daughter-in-law. You must let me do it."

"Even if *your* conscience would be satisfied, *mine* would not as your mother-in-law. And since I was the first to speak, I insist on being the first."

The exchange continued with the same phrases repeated over and over. At last, Seishu could no longer tolerate the double-entendres and threw himself on his bed. He bellowed like a wild beast and awakened the household.

"Stop! Stop! Stop!"

He scolded his wife, and then said to his mother, "Mother, you said you don't have many years to live and that you don't care for your life. Are you really so sure you would die if you took my medicine?" He glowered in anger. The women were silent. Carried away with their desire for credit, they had completely ignored Seishu's ego and pride.

"Forgive me," apologized Kae immediately.

"It was silly of me to say such things. Forgive me too," said his regretful mother.

Seishu quickly resumed his mild, easy manner and tried to persuade the women to go away. "Come now. Restrain yourselves and go to sleep. I'm getting sleepy too."

But they were still unyielding and would not leave. Otsugi was facing her son, trying once again to convince him.

107

"If you're so confident, why do you hesitate to use me?"

"Oh no, it should be me," interrupted Kae.

"I won't let my daughter-in-law do it."

"Why not? If my husband used his own mother, what would people think of him?"

"How could he be blamed if I volunteer?"

"Still, it's up to me," insisted Kae.

"Are you going to oppose your own mother-in-law?"

"That depends. Under the circumstances, I don't think it would go against my duty."

After that, the mother and daughter-in-law proceeded to argue with more and more ardor. Each fought to protect the other, avowing willingly to sacrifice her own life and concealing daggers in her words. During this noble exchange of sentiments, both women were completely carried away.

Seishu stated that his medicine would not cause death. Neither woman doubted his word. Mafutsu, after all, had recently executed a fine spin in the air and hadn't died. But he didn't run and play in the yard either. He merely lay in the sun, dozing lazily with hardly a glance at any mice that appeared, and a cat who doesn't run after mice is strange. There were many such cats and dogs, who, having taken the drug, moved like ghosts in and out of the house.

Seishu was becoming disheartened watching his mother and wife unleash their "noble" arguments. But he knew he shouldn't interfere. The deep-rooted feud between the woman who bore him and the one who would bear his children could not be settled with a surgical knife. Gradually, however, he began to view their conversation from a scientist's perspective. Suppose the medicine were administered to a human being. The dangers, of course, were great, as there were no records indicating what might happen. Eventually the doctor was so absorbed with his inner thoughts that he neither saw nor heard the women quarreling.

"Yes, I see." His entire body seemed to have reached a decision, and his eyes sparkled when he spoke again. The thick eyebrows expressed an underlying determination to follow his scientific inclinations; the mole on his throat did not budge.

"Well, then," he continued, "I will engage both of you for my experiment. I have to try it on someone someday."

At that moment Kae felt like collapsing. All of her energy was drained and she felt dizzy. Otsugi, as if to have the last word, insisted, "If you want two of us, then let me be the first."

The three agreed that the experiment would remain a secret, not to be shared even with the students. Koriku was informed that her mother was going to be treated for an old, neglected ailment. Only Seishu, Otsugi, and Kae knew the truth.

Seishu needed time to prepare a dosage that he considered proper. One month passed. The day before he was ready, Otsugi carefully combed her hair many times before washing it. Kae thought of assisting her, but when she saw Otsugi at the well, she was too shocked by the shortness of her hair to offer to help. The thick, black hair which had always been her mother-in-law's source of pride must have stopped growing and was now only shoulder-length. Just two years ago, on Otsugi's sixtieth birthday, Kae remembered there had not been a hint of gray in it. Wondering how the color stayed a lovely jet-black, Kae imagined that she used to pull out the gray strands. It was amazing that her hair had not aged, unlike her own, which contained some gray no matter how often she pulled out the offending hairs. But now it was so short! The younger woman trembled as she considered her mother-in-law's age and her present courage in spite of it.

Otsugi washed her hair several times, letting it float in a bowl of warm water mixed with the juice of the Japanese magnolia blossom and starch. The hair floated and coiled around Otsugi's hands as she washed it. Kae watched but still didn't move. It was an ominous scene, resembling a preparation for death. For despite Seishu's assurances, Otsugi calmly assumed the worst. Solemnly, Kae examined her own position should Otsugi die and she survive. Kae knew that in such a case she would hear the villagers praising her mother-in-law for the rest of her days. But she was next in line, and someday soon it would be her turn to wash her hair. The thought was frightening. As she looked at Otsugi's back, she could distinctly sense her strong determination to make Kae follow her to the other world. Kae wondered if there existed another woman comparable to Otsugi, one who could wash her hair under similar conditions without the slightest trace of anxiety.

Koriku was bringing another bucketful of hot water, and alongside her ran a spotted dog named Kiba. Refusing to watch Otsugi any longer, Kae was about to return to the house when Kiba barked at her feet. No sooner had she taken a step than she felt something soft under her right foot, and Kiba jumped squealing. Kae instantly moved back, but it was too late. The dog whirled around and around so fast that his spots merged with the white on his back. He then let out a shrill cry and fell to the ground. Blood gushed from his mouth.

Koriku screamed and covered her face with her hands. The bucket fell to the ground and water flowed over her feet. Stupified, Kae's body stiffened as she stared at the dog who had just died. She couldn't believe her eyes!

"Kae, what have you done! What a cruel thing to do, and on this day!" The pale face with dripping wet hair hurled the sort of accusations that helped Kae recover her senses.

The following morning, Kae arranged Otsugi's bedding in Seishu's room. Her mother-in-law rested quietly on a mattress. She was in her nightclothes, and her clean, carefully oiled hair hung loosely around her shoulders. It was customary for a sick woman to let her hair down in case the pillow slipped out from under her head. To avoid appearing disheveled, Otsugi had tied a light green silk ribbon around her hair and across her forehead. Commonly called a "sick person's ribbon," it was tied at the upper left temple, the ends falling unevenly to one side of her face.

Seishu himself mixed the dose. There were only the three of them in the room—Kae, Otsugi, and Seishu. Otsugi held a large teacup and inquired of her son in a soft voice, "How long before it takes effect?"

"I think it depends on the individual, but I assume less than an hour."

"Really?"

Seishu and Kae watched her drink the contents, with the sublime expression of a martyr on her face.

"It wasn't as bitter as I expected."

"I added a sweetener to make it easier."

"It's wonderful if a person can go to sleep by just taking a drink."

"Please, lie down immediately and stay still. The medicine is quite potent."

"I will. But before I do, I have something to ask you."

"What's that, Mother?"

"When Ryohei comes home, I want you to adopt him as your son."

"You mean my own brother?"

"Yes. I'm worried because the Hanaokas have no heir Not that I dream of dying from this delicious medicine. But this has been on my mind for some time. Please, make Ryohei your heir."

"All right, Mother. Since he is also studying medicine, he will be a very capable successor."

"Now I feel better."

She lay on the bed for a while and tried to fix her hair and the ribbon so that she would not look unattractive in bed. Soon she closed her eyes as she was told.

"If your stomach starts to ache, let me know right away. Kae or I will stay by your bed."

Otsugi merely nodded. She may have been trying to conserve her energy, and for that reason suppressed any emotion. Yet to Kae, she seemed comical, like an actress in a performance. The woman who peered at her yesterday through wet hair and this gracious old lady in silent meditation were like two different people. If one looked hard, there were a few noticeable wrinkles around her eyes, but one had to admit that she was still beautiful for her age. By comparison to Kae's own mother who had died two years before, Otsugi looked very young. Kae often wondered what the secret was of her youth and beauty.

Some patients arrived and Seishu disappeared, leaving the women alone. The medicine did not work quickly. A heavy silence filled the room. Otsugi rested with her eyes shut and Kae did not speak. Until very recently, a few dogs and cats, sometimes more than a few, had been lying on the straw matted floor. Now they were gone. And only the sound of the two women breathing broke the absolute silence. But the past experiments had left a variety of odors: animal, medicinal, fishy, and the stench of vomit, blood, and decay—a suffocating combination, like the reek of dead bodies. Kae stared at the sleeping face. She almost ceased to blink as she wondered

112

whether the smell of Otsugi's body would soon be mingled with the other odors.

Otsugi's last wish was also very much on her mind, although she tried hard to cast it aside. She regarded her mother-in-law's request that Seishu adopt his own brother as a final declaration against her, since it clearly implied that Otsugi intended to eliminate Kae and her blood line from the Hanaoka family. How she regretted the careless manner in which she expressed her feelings of inferiority for not having produced a male child during their last quarrel? Why, Seishu might easily adopt Koben's future husband as his heir. Biting her lip, she thought with bitterness back to the days when she had been wanted, and she glared at the sleeping woman. Wasn't it obvious that Otsugi now hated her? Why else did she submit to the experiment—except as a means of bringing up an issue that would make her uncomfortable? Or as a means of compelling her daughter-in-law to share her fate?

But Kae had Koben. "Who," she wondered, "would care for the little girl until she married in the event something happened to me?" Kae shuddered at what might be in store for her poor child in such a case.

Otsugi's white cheeks turned pink and she began to breathe more rapidly. Opening her eyes slightly, she saw that Kae was observing her and closed them—almost as an automatic reflex. It seemed as if she were trying to bear pain. Kae had been instructed to inform her husband if there were any changes in Otsugi's condition, so she hurried off to find him.

The doctor felt his mother's pulse and asked if she were in pain.

"No," she replied, "but my body feels hot, everywhere."

"That's normal with this medicine. Don't worry, Mother."

"I wasn't. I didn't call you. It was Kae who went to get you."

The house was full of patients, some coming from very far away for treatment. Usually they stayed in private homes in and around Hirayama so that they could see Seishu every day until they were cured. The doctor returned to the examination room.,

A quarter of an hour later, Otsugi was writhing in pain. But she shook off Kae's hands abruptly, groaned, and arched her body. Her pillow fell to one side. Then kicking off the covers, she began to scratch wildly at her breasts. Seishu entered just as Kae was about to look for him.

"Mother, Mother!" he called, pinning her by the shoulders. Otsugi seemed to have heard him. Her eyes were all red.

"Umpei?"

"Does it hurt, Mother?"

"Not too much. I feel like moving around. The pain is tolerable."

"It's going to be all right."

"Umpei?" repeated Otsugi.

"What is it, Mother?"

"Umpei, you are my child, aren't you?"

"Of course I am."

"You are mine only, Umpei?"

"That's right," he answered laughingly, as if he were indulging a small child. When his mother calmed down, he returned to his patients.

Otsugi continued to have difficulty breathing, and from time to time went into short convulsions. Looking at her, Kae thought only of the scene that had just transpired—how in her ravings and clouded consciousness, Otsugi asserted that her son belonged to her alone and not to his wife. Otsugi's delirium reminded Kae of Koben's birth, the intensity of the sharp pains that required all of her strength, almost her life. It is said that the

114

discomforts of the first delivery are the worst, which is why they are generally remembered. Perhaps that was the reason Otsugi felt Seishu to be more precious to her than her other children and tried to monopolize his affections, reasoned Kae, as she regained her composure. Kae felt at ease with Otsugi only when she thought of some common experience they shared, like producing a Hanaoka child. She had tried to bury their feud after Okatsu's death and show her mother-in-law some sympathy. But her attempts went unappreciated at that time, and in fact, their distance increased afterwards. Otsugi was as critical toward her as ever.

Her mother-in-law fell into a deep coma. Kae felt remorseful and dispelled her angry and bitter thoughts. She even felt pity for this poor creature who needed to believe that Seishu was hers alone. Maybe Otsugi would die. Or maybe she would be left a vegetable like the dogs and cats. Absorbed in her imaginings, Kae lost all her rancor for a time.

Otsugi's relaxed body barely moved, and her complexion regained its porcelain, milky color. Kae took her pulse. It was normal. In her sleep, her will to reject her daughter-in-law also became dormant.

"Mother!" whispered Kae into Otsugi's ear. No response. Perhaps her hearing had also been affected.

In her frenzy Otsugi's nightgown had come undone, exposing her shriveled breasts, so scrawny that they appeared like two weak living things against the bright blue nightgown and white skin. Kae tidied the nightgown, neatly closed the front, and straightened her legs, which were spread wide apart.

About noon, the anesthetic seemed to be in full effect. Kae informed Seishu, who only looked in briefly to say that he was going off to lunch. Surprised by the coolness of his reaction,

Kae asked, "Are you sure she's all right? She was rolling around frantically. Won't there be bad effects later?"

"There's no danger at all," he replied casually. "Though I put a bit of *mandarage* in the drink, I added an antidote. Besides, there wasn't any *uzu* in it. The medicine was mixed in saké, so she drank nothing more than a strong alcoholic beverage. Now she's just sleeping off the drunkenness."

Kae's disappointment was evident, and because she regretted her earlier sympathy, she became angry and despondent again. Without the extremely poisonous *uzu*, she knew that her mother-in-law would recover. Thinking once more of Otsugi's possessiveness toward Seishu, her hostility was easily rekindled. She was sorry she had closed Otsugi's nightgown, for had her mother-in-law been left in that unsightly state, how ashamed that stupid, pretentious woman would have felt!

Seishu ate a leisurely lunch, and then returned to his mother.

"Mother, Mother," he called loudly.

There was no answer. Kae had carefully rearranged Otsugi's ribbon some time ago.

"There . . . she moved," he murmured. Kae wondered about the actual contents of the concoction. Was it really as simple as Seishu had described?

Removing the covers, Seishu opened the bottom of his mother's nightgown. Kae was dismayed, but watched, eager to find out what was going to happen next. Seishu's fingers groped around his mother's inner thigh and stopped.

"Oooh," groaned Otsugi, stirring finally, after Seishu pinched the most sensitive part of her body.

"She's weak as I expected. But in less than half an hour she'll probably open her eyes and move by herself. Call me then." He returned to his patients once more.

Kae was too upset with him to answer. How could he, her

own husband, have put his hands on another woman's private parts while his own wife looked on? Remembering her intimate evenings with him, she felt as if her body were a piece of wood that had been planed against the grain. Even though she was soon able to rationalize that it was only his mother, and that he was a doctor who had pinched his patient to find out whether she was asleep, no amount of justification could pacify her. How could he have done it? Otsugi remained asleep, as if nothing had happened. That serene face looked so smug. Maybe she wasn't really unconscious. Maybe she knew all along that her son was poking around her thighs while his wife watched. Kae soon convinced herself that Otsugi was aware of everything and had only pretended to be asleep. She couldn't reason any other way.

As predicted, Otsugi woke up in less than thirty minutes. Looking around, she seemed groggy, but upon noticing Kae, asked very softly, "How long have I been asleep?"

"Around an hour."

"Really. I had no idea. So the medicine worked!" In apparent contentment, she closed her eyes again.

Kae wanted to shout that the drink contained none of the dangerous drugs, that the experiment was still incomplete, and that she had been aroused merely by a pinch and not with a probe. But Seishu was next door. And, of course, Kae couldn't have spoken that way in any case.

When Seishu learned that his mother had awakened, he immediately came in with a bowl.

"Mother?"

"Yes, dear. Is the experiment over?"

"Yes, Mother, it's finished. Don't you have a headache?"

"No."

"Can you see well?"

"Why not?"

"So everything's all right. Sit up now and take this."

Eyeing the bowl in his hand, Otsugi tried to sit, but couldn't. Kae approached her from behind to assist. And Otsugi, who seemed satisfied for some unknown reason, did not object and let Kae's arms support her whole weight.

"Another medicine?"

"No, just a tonic, like a strong cup of tea. It may taste bitter, but you'll be fine in no time at all."

Otsugi drank it in several gulps. After perspiring so much during her high fever, she seemed thirsty. Her smile was radiant as she addressed her son. "I'm fine. Wasn't it a tremendous success, Umpei?"

"Yes, Mother, thanks to you." Seishu lowered his head.

Kae felt like laughing, but if she had, she was sure she would not have been able to stop for a day or two. Moreover, it would have been impolite to laugh at her mother-in-law in front of her husband, and she didn't want to offend him. So she, too, lowered her head and feigned an air of modesty.

Seishu ordered his mother to stay in bed for two or three days and to begin eating a thin porridge, slowly to be switched to regular food by the time she could get up. Loud noises interrupted his orders and Seishu left; an emergency case may have been brought in. Otsugi lay down and called for Kae. It had been many years since she had spoken to her daughter-in-law in such a sweet, gentle voice.

"I'm sure you're relieved. Now you see there's nothing to worry about. Perhaps you won't have to take the medicine at all."

Do you think so? thought Kae to herself, her restraint nearly shattered. What a sense of superiority she has! It crossed her mind to say, "You old woman, you didn't take anything powerful. Seishu himelf told me so. The real experiment will be on me, I'm sure." But Kae kept her mouth shut and answered pleasantly, "Yes, it's a great relief to know that you're well."

XI

The experiment was supposed to be kept secret between the three of them. But, either out of pride or elation, Otsugi told Koriku and Yonejiro, who within ten days informed the students. Thereafter, the courageous mother of the doctor was held in great reverence and esteem. Meanwhile, the aura around Otsugi began to affect Kae so that whenever she was alone with her husband she implored him to use her as a subject.

"Mother doesn't know anything. But she's telling everybody of your success. Pretty soon, you'll be in quite an embarrassing position. Suppose the anesthetic is requested for an operation? What will you do then?"

"Ummm . . . " he seemed troubled by his mother's hastily formed conclusion that his research was completed.

"I'll do anything to protect your reputation, even if I have to take a strong dosage of your medicine. You can hardly call waking up from a pinch a true test, can you? Remember, neither Byakusen nor Kiba moved or made a sound when the probe entered their bodies. Well, what do you say?"

"Ummm . . . I used only ten percent of *mandarage* and no *byakushi* or *uzu*. I think perhaps a mixture of eighty percent *mandarage* and twenty percent *uzu* will work on a human being."

"Then, please try it on me!"

"Umm . . . " Seishu continued to hesitate, and his wife to insist. Gradually, scientific exigencies and personal ambitions surmounted human considerations, and six months later Seishu undertook the second, really the first, experiment. His drug contained a large quantity of *mandarage* (*Datura alba* Nees—the flowers as well as the seeds), a smaller amount of the poisonous *uzu* (*Tuber aconiti*), some *byakushi* (*Angelica grabrae*), *senkyu* (*Cnidium officinale* M)—certainly nothing like the preparation given to Otsugi. Seishu wrote the name and quantity of each ingredient on one side of his pad, left the opposite side a blank in order to record his wife's reactions, and placed it near the bed with the empty page in view.

Not that Kae wanted to imitate her mother-in-law, but the day before the experiment she washed her hair. In the relaxing autumnal sunshine she remembered the disappointment on Otsugi's face when she was told by her son after six months had gone by that she, Kae, would be his next subject. Koben was helping to undo her mother's long thick hair (which still could not be compared to Otsugi's). It was washed and rinsed several times. As she lathered the ends, the ten-year-old commented innocently, "What long hair you have! I wonder when mine will be like yours."

Imagining this might be a farewell between them, Kae was overcome with melancholy; her tears flowed easily.

"Why are you crying?"

"Water got into my eyes." Then, thinking she had heard a rustle behind her, she asked her daughter if someone were there, to which Koben replied, "Yes, Grandma's been watching you."

The realization that Otsugi had seen her tears provoked Kae's fighting spirit and encouraged her to exhibit a strong motherly image to her daughter.

Apart from washing her hair, Kae took other precautions. She skipped dinner that night, believing that the drug would act quicker on an empty stomach and that she would be less likely to vomit. And the next day, after binding her knees and ankles together with some pieces of cloth bandage, she covered her legs with her nightgown. She had learned much from her grandmother, who had formerly served at the castle and therefore, besides knowing how to use a small sword, could make a special knot that was employed in the samurai manner of committing suicide. Her grandmother used to tell her that the harder one struggled, the more constricting the knot became. So, in samurai fashion, Kae methodically fixed her legs and tied a long sash several times over her nightwear and around her waist, tucking the ends under. It was reassuring to feel that her mother-in-law would not have to straighten her kimono once the drug was operative, though if Otsugi saw her delirious, she would surely visualize how she herself must have behaved during her own experiment.

Kae was ready to accept the drink from her husband. The licorice sweetener had been added for flavoring this time as well. Still, it was bitter.

"Hold your breath and drink up. It will go down more smoothly," advised Otsugi as one experienced in the matter.

Kae simply frowned and swallowed the liquid in three gulps,

constraining herself from revealing that the contents of her beverage were quite different from those in her mother-in-law's drink. Almost immediately she felt a strange sensation on her tongue and throat, and her voice grew muffled.

"Want some water?"

Kae nodded. Her tongue and throat burned.

"Mother, please get her a cup of water."

Otsugi left at once and returned with the water. It was obviously unpleasant for her to wait on her daughter-in-law.

Seishu had not been nearly so thoughtful toward Otsugi, thought Kae, although feeling as she did, this knowledge gave her little satisfaction. She drank like a thirsty animal and then groaned. In her deteriorating condition, she did not consider a last testament. A fierce heat raged inside her stomach and she could feel her flushed face and ears, as if the blood were racing all over her body.

"Koben, Koben . . . " she gasped, looking at her husband.

"What is it?"

"Please take care of her."

"Don't be silly. You won't die."

"Still . . . please . . . Koben."

"I know."

"Please, Koben is your child."

"All right."

In her fading consciousness, the suffering face was fixed on the large black mole of the man who leaned toward her. It did not enter her mind that Otsugi was present and that her remark concerning Koben had been misconstrued. But there was no doubt that Otsugi thought Kae was making a counter to her own request for Seishu's adoption of Ryohei. Subconsciously of course, the rivalry might indeed have motivated Kae's concern for Koben.

Kae's reactions to the drug were faster than Otsugi's. Her body aflame, she cried aloud in a frenzy of continuous screams, unaware that she was frightening the patients in the other rooms. Nor did she know that Shimomura Ryoan of Myoji temple had been called to take over for Seishu so that he would not have to leave her room at all. The high fever and delirium lasted several hours until she fell into a deep sleep.

For three days and two nights while Kae lay inert, Seishu took her pulse, recorded detailed notes, and prepared a black bean broth for an antidote. His bed was brought in and placed next to his wife's, but he remained awake and kept a steady vigil at her side. Otsugi herself did not change into her nightclothes. Day and night she observed her slumbering daughter-in-law and her son whose eyes had become very red from lack of sleep.

Ryoan had not visited the Hanaokas since Okatsu's death, and was truly happy with the invitation to return to his teacher's house. But his joy was short-lived. Upon learning what Seishu had done, he turned ashen. Because of his familiarity with drugs in general, he could conjecture about the contents of Seishu's anesthetic based on the information given by Yonejiro. But now that Kae had already taken it, there was no way he could stop the experiment. He was surprised by the courage and capacity for self-sacrifice in this simple, ordinary woman whom he thought he knew, having been a resident with the Hanaokas even before Kae's entry into the family. And when he heard that she had actually volunteered to be Seishu's subject, his astonishment was even greater.

Early on the morning of the third day, Ryoan felt compelled to speak to Otsugi, whom he saw coming out of the room.

"She's been asleep for a long time. Going without food for three days is very debilitating, you know. Unless Kae is awakened and fed, I fear some disaster may befall her." He would never have spoken thus to a bleary, red-eyed Seishu.

"Well, Kae may be content to die, but I would be greatly distressed if this happened. I, more than anyone, pray for her recovery. Umpei has definite ideas, and I cannot intrude with mine, but I'm heartbroken. You see, when I took the drug I woke up after an hour or so. Perhaps Kae is overly sensitive to the anesthetic and the experiment will be spoiled. How I pray for her well-being! Had the test been repeated on me alone, as I urged, I don't think I would have suffered as I do now. But she didn't listen. Ryoan, please praise her for what she did and pray for her. Pray that she lives through this. For if something should happen to this daughter-in-law whom I especially requested from the distinguished family of Nate, I would not be able to go on living, even though I'm afraid she hasn't been a good wife for my son."

Ryoan could not believe his ears, for from her manner of speech, he concluded that Otsugi was agonizing over the fate of her daughter-in-law whom she herself had chosen for her son. As he was often troubled by the petty quarreling that persisted between his own mother and wife, the existence of a harmonious relationship among the Hanaoka women had particularly impressed him. It seemed indeed rare and beautiful to find a mother and wife fighting to be used in an experiment. So he bowed to Otsugi and suggested that she rest in another room.

"Please, you are terribly tired. Go and lie down," he urged her gently. "Of course we are all worried about the doctor's wife, but if you, the doctor's mother, should become ill, it will be even more serious."

"Oh, no. How can I lie down or think of sleeping? Although I don't know anything about science, I want to join my son and pray for his success. You understand, I am his mother. Yet I wonder why he gave his wife a dosage that has put her to sleep for three days when he had been so successful with me!" Her voice suddenly rose to a higher pitch. "I just can't bear watching him test the drug on her."

"Why? Did he use a probe?" inquired the agitated Ryoan. Recalling that the animals had been prodded with such tools many times, he suspected that Kae might be sharing their fate, and his face darkened.

"No, it's not that."

"Well then, what is he using?"

"It's not a probe." She explained no further and left.

Ryoan felt utterly helpless but did not try to comprehend Otsugi's strange behavior.

Both Otsugi and Seishu were so exhausted and overwrought that they couldn't eat or sleep. Seishu continued to peer intently into his wife's face and neither heard nor saw his students when they greeted him each morning. His patients were not supposed to know what was going on, though undoubtedly they felt the tension that pervaded the house. Toward evening on the third day, Kae opened her eyes just a bit.

"Kae, are you conscious?" asked Seishu quietly, suppressing his joy.

The expressionless face nodded and the eyes closed again. Still in a stupor, she did not move. Her legs and head seemed bound to the bed.

Seishu refused to permit anyone in the room, so only Otsugi, sitting at the far end of the bed facing both him and Kae, was present. She noted her son's expression, with a mixture of complex feelings. For if the experiment should fail on account of Kae's death, the consequences would be far-reaching, much greater than they had been with the animals. Just as the tide recedes, patients would no longer come. And at the worst, Seishu would be punished and the dream of the Hanaokas irrevocably terminated. Obsessed by these fears, Otsugi had prayed for Kae to regain consciousness and had begged Ryoan to do the same. But whenever Seishu pinched his wife's thigh to test the anesthetic, feelings of jealousy raged within her and, at these moments, she hated Kae sufficiently to wish for her death. It was these sorts of contradictions that inhabited Otsugi's tortured mind when Kae finally started to awaken. Although she leaned forward to see her, Otsugi found it impossible to join in her son's happiness as he called to his wife. Soon, however, her face turned whiter than ever. Seishu was transmitting the antidote from his own mouth into Kae's.

The patient was ingesting a black bean broth very slowly, not realizing that she was sipping it out of her husband's mouth. When her numbed tongue moved between his lips, Seishu responded with his own, repeating this act of love many times in front of his stupified mother until the large bowl of broth was consumed. Contented, Kae fell asleep once more.

Again Seishu felt Kae's pulse. His face radiated out of sheer happiness and he addressed his mother like a small boy reporting his accomplishments.

"Mother, she's all right! Thank goodness it's over. She'll be alert in less than half an hour."

Looking at the monstrous black stains on his mouth, Otsugi broke out into goose bumps.

"Please cook your tasty rice porridge and give her three egg yolks. Kae hasn't eaten for three days."

"Neither have you," replied his mother in a ruffled voice.

"Right. Then I'll eat here with her."

"The same thing?"

"Porridge is best after a fast. Kae has to get her strength back

quickly. I'll have some eggs too. And we'll have them raw."
Jubilation flowed spontaneously from his heart.

A beaten Otsugi headed for the kitchen. How different he
had been when she woke up! She dropped two handfuls of rice
in a pot, wondering why she had not been invited to join them.
After all, she had also gone without nourishment. Tears filled
her eyes as she washed the rice by the well, careful not to spill
a single grain. Her misery seemed too much for her. The
picture of Seishu's hand in his wife's kimono and the oral
transfer of broth had been indelibly imprinted on her memory.

Yonejiro passed by. Seldom did anyone see Otsugi washing
rice if Koriku and the maids were around. Besides, it was well
known that this woman, who always protected her hands,
disliked washing and scrubbing. And why was she weeping
and shaking her shoulders that way?

"What's the matter?" asked Yonejiro.

"Kae woke up," answered the sobbing woman when she
finally perceived Yonejiro. "Umpei is so happy. He said they'll
eat porridge together. Together!"

Yonejiro rushed to the students' quarters with the news.
"The doctor's wife has just awakened. The experiment
worked. And his mother is weeping for joy—preparing porridge and washing rice while tears stream down her cheeks."

Everyone got up. Shimomura Ryoan, who was the eldest,
was also the first to speak.

"Really? That's marvelous! It's so wonderful. They are both
model women. Each has risked her life to help the doctor
achieve his dreams."

No one disagreed. All nodded and silence ensued. At last,
Nakagawa Shutei said what was on his mind.

"To be unconscious for three days! Isn't that too long? Can
the patient really recover?"

No one dared reply. They were all certain, judging from Seishu's character, that his research on humans was not over. Consequently, they were not entirely ready for a celebration.

Seishu, on the other hand, was extremely excited as he fed his wife some porridge while he himself noisily devoured his food.

"Did you dream? . . . No? . . . Is that right?" Because Kae was still unable to move any part of her body except for her eyes, Seishu asked questions to which he himself replied, taking notes on his pad in between feeding Kae spoonfuls of porridge mixed with egg. "Do you have a headache? . . . Was it painful? . . . Really? . . . How do you feel? . . . Groggy? Sleepy? Can you move? . . . No, don't. Your legs must feel like lead. Can you lift them? No. . . don't try so hard. Your muscles ache? . . . No? . . . Is that right?"

Although she had less of an appetite than Seishu, Kae was so pleased with his attentiveness that she allowed all of five tea-spoonfuls of porridge and one egg yolk to slide down her throat. Besides, she wanted to show off in front of her mother-in-law. If she could have, she would have eaten more.

"By the way, Kae, where did you learn to tie such a knot?" Having finished his notes, Seishu could relax, so he changed the subject.

Kae knew that he had seen her legs and felt somewhat shy, although, of course, she expected the question.

"Don't try answering. You might get a headache."

"No, it's all right," she said, her voice weak. "I learned it from my grandmother, as part of the training of a samurai's daughter."

"What is it called?"

"I don't know. But she told me that no matter how much one moved, the knot would only become tighter."

"Let me try it."

Seishu looked back at his mother and asked for some string. Otsugi thought of offering her sash but changed her mind. She was about to leave for her own room when she changed her mind again, took off her sash, and tied her waist with another sash which she lifted out of a wicker basket.

With the band still warm from Otsugi's body, Seishu threw his legs near Kae's pillow and tried to bind them together at the knees.

"Like this? Now am I supposed to tie it again here?"

Instead of a common knot which is made by turning one end of a string around another and then repeating the process but reversing the ends, one end is turned around the other twice; both ends are pulled in reverse directions, and are then tucked in. Now there is a tie, but no knot, and it doesn't come apart easily.

Seishu was fascinated. He loosened his kimono and tied and untied it over and over, like a child absorbed in a new toy.

"Mother, it seems so trivial. But really, it's clever. Caspar didn't teach this. Simple! Practical too! And it can be used to stop bleeding. Ingenious! Only a samurai woman would think of it."

Otsugi responded to his childish enthusiasm with a graceful smile. "Indeed it is!" she replied. She felt refreshed and her old self again, full of strength and confidence, due undoubtedly to her sudden determination and belief that her turn was next.

Almost half a month passed before Kae's health returned to normal. And it was seven days before she could even go to the bathroom by herself. Otsugi looked after her with much devotion. Since it was obviously a painful experience, Kae often declined her assistance and told Otsugi that Koben would help her. But the elderly woman refused to hear of it. She became indescribably tender and told Kae during several conversations that she had prayed for her safety. No one in the house imagined that a kinder, more gentle mother-in-law than Otsugi could be found anywhere.

"Did I really sleep for three days?" Kae asked her.

"Yes."

"But you got up within a few hours. I'm sorry you had to worry about me. Truly, I'm very sorry."

The words had been carefully chosen, as Kae hoped to discover whether Otsugi suspected that the medications had been different. But Otsugi was not the least offended. Nor had she any difficulty parrying her daughter-in-law's remark because she was already looking forward to playing a bigger role in the next experiment.

Everyone thought both women were most congenial and understanding to one another. But the vehemence of their rivalry and mutual hatred, which had no outlet in words or deeds, was increasing. Was such a relationship unavoidable between any mother and daughter-in-law? Perhaps. However, in this case, the clash was surely aggravated by the people surrounding the two women. Seishu's students, for example, who visited Kae during her recovery, did not hold back their praise and esteem for her in front of Otsugi, who until three days before had been the only recipient of such admiration. Sensing Otsugi's gradual coldness, Kae wished to be on her own as quickly as possible to escape the icy touch of her mother-in-law's hands.

When she was finally able to walk to the toilet by herself, Kae examined her whole body and saw the blue bruises from the bands below her knees and ankles, evidence of wild, unconscious behavior. And sure enough, when she peeped at her inner thigh which had been bothering her ever since she woke up, there were fingermarks—three purplish red circles edged in yellow. Seishu had tested the anesthetic in the same place. He had dared to put his hand on his wife's thigh in front of his mother!

She smelled the odors around the toilet bowl and choked, reeled, and lost her balance, staggering toward the opposite wall. Then she fell with a thud. Koriku rushed in to see if she was all right. The pale Kae managed a beleaguered smile and said that she was, failing to notice that her sister-in-law was staring at her as if she had been frightened by something terrible. Kae, however, was satisfied that she had outdone Otsugi and did not mind her weakened condition, although she did not recover her strength for some time.

XII

The first day of spring arrived. Alone at the well, an elated Kae welcomed the cool water running over her chapped hands. From time to time while she scrubbed the clothes, she grinned and chuckled over the recollection of some of the humorous events in her life, the most recent being a conversation that had taken place with Otsugi earlier that morning. Seishu had gone off to the local inn to see a patient whose condition had suddenly deteriorated, so only Kae was present when Otsugi awakened from the medication she had taken the previous day.

"How long have I slept?" she asked.

"Oh, are you awake? How do you feel?" replied Kae, testing the temperature of the cup of tea in her hands.

But Otsugi quietly repeated her question, confident that she had slept longer than Kae had under the same anesthetic. "How many days have passed?"

Kae hesitated. It would have pleased her to be blunt, to say "only overnight," but she managed to restrain the impulse. She knew that the drug Seishu had prepared for his mother was intended to produce a fast reaction, but that it had not contained any of the ferocious *uzu*. Consequently, Otsugi was indeed quick to fall asleep. However, without *uzu* it was obvious to everyone that the anesthetic would not be strong enough; in fact, each time Seishu pinched her arm, Otsugi moved. And because there was no real cause for concern, the doctor felt free to leave the house when he had to. His mother, of course, had no way of knowing that she had taken nothing more than a powerful sleeping potion. In Kae's opinion the experiment had been undertaken only to please and appease Otsugi, who had insisted that she be used for further tests.

Kae's answer was carefully worded. "I don't know how long it's been. I feel very tired because I've been up the whole time. Really, I can't remember how many days. I'm awfully sorry."

Otsugi seemed unsatisfied; the look on her face accused Kae of stupidity, but she didn't voice her feelings. Instead she said rather gently, "I'm sorry to have made you worry. Please take a nap. I'm all right now."

"Oh, don't fret over me. Here, drink this tea. It's an antidote."

"Where's Umpei?" asked Otsugi angrily, as she began to recall her son's mouth-to-mouth administration of the antidote to his wife, while she now had to hold the cup by herself.

"He went to the inn on an emergency call."

She shrugged off Kae's supporting hands and gulped the hot tea down. Evidently it was bitter and left an unpleasant taste. She frowned and lay down again, resuming the conversation a little later on.

"Don't you think that this experiment, unlike the last one,

was a great success? I'm not as weak as you were, so I probably won't have to stay in bed."

"Aren't you tired?"

"Well, of course, I feel a bit faint from not eating. But I'm much stronger than you were."

"Yes, it seems that way. Only you could have gone through it. I'm ashamed of myself."

"I didn't mean anything like that. The difference in our reactions is because the anesthetic has undoubtedly been improved. Just be happy for Umpei."

"I certainly am. And he will also be very pleased. Now, don't you think you ought to get some rest?"

"All right. It wouldn't do for the subject of such an important experiment to be too talkative." And with a sense of satisfaction, she closed her eyes and drifted into a peaceful slumber.

Seishu returned not long afterwards. Hearing his footsteps, Kae slipped out of the room to greet him.

"I'm glad you're back. Mother just woke up."

"Good."

"She was telling me what a big success this experiment was."

"Why is that?"

"Well, unlike me, she said she felt strong."

"That's natural."

"What shall I prepare for her meal?"

"Some plain porridge will do, I think."

Kae cooked some rice on the kitchen stove and then went outdoors to do the laundry. Dozing only occasionally, she had remained awake all of the previous night, watching her husband sleeping by his mother's side. Now, as she washed and rinsed the clothes in the fresh water, she felt as if she had just awakened from a sound night's sleep.

She was sure that Otsugi would also ask her son how long the anesthetic had been effective and that Seishu would probably not have enough consideration to lie. The doctor was known to be rather insensitive and often a bit brusque with his patients. Kae could imagine him saying, "Mother, it was only yesterday afternoon that you took the medicine."

Having undone the seams of one of Koben's kimonos, so that each piece of material could be washed and stretched, Kae called for her sister-in-law.

"Koriku, would you please give Mother porridge, a pickled plum, and an egg yolk? I'm sure she'd prefer to have you serve her. I've got to finish stretching these materials on the boards before it gets too dark."

"Did you say before it gets too dark?" repeated a dubious Koriku, for it was a sunny day, in fact, an exceptionally bright one for early spring. Had Kae had many garments to do, Koriku would have understood. But she saw only a few things in the basin, all of them easily finished by noon.

"Yes, before dark. I thought it was a nice day. But now it seems to be getting cloudy, and I'll have to hurry to get these done." Kae failed to observe Koriku's wide-eyed, skeptical expression.

"Sister . . ." Koriku began to say something, caught herself, and asked, "Did you say porridge, a plum, and an egg yolk?" After receiving confirmation, she headed for the house.

Another odd thing happened to Koriku when she brought her mother a tray of food.

"When did I take the medicine?" Otsugi asked her daughter.

"Probably yesterday afternoon."

"Really?" Otsugi looked puzzled.

"Why should I lie to you?"

"You and Umpei both said yesterday, so it must be true."

"Why do you ask, Mother?"

"Kae said that I had slept a long time, so long that she lost count of the days."

Koriku didn't say a word. Tears of resentment and frustration streamed down her mother's cheeks.

XIII

A few months later, toward the beginning of summer, Koben died. An ordinary cold turned into pneumonia, and in a short while the little girl was gone, as a child who might have disappeared in pursuit of a butterfly in a grassy field. During the month and a half prior to her death, Kae had been completely withdrawn yet aware that an increasing darkness was surrounding her, which she attributed to the light in her life gradually fading into extinction. Finally, at the sight of Koben in her tiny coffin, she was overcome with grief; the parting was difficult. After the cremation and the burial of a small urn under the Hanaoka gravestone near the Iris Pond, she burst into a mournful wail.

"No one can share the suffering of a mother who must outlive her own child, except another mother who has had the same misfortune," she cried, her tears rolling freely over Otsugi's shoulder.

"Cry as long as possible, Kae. If you can, you're better off. It's when your tears stop falling that the loneliness becomes intolerable, and you'll want to tear yourself to pieces. Ever since Okatsu died, not a day has passed when I haven't wished to join her."

"The same may happen to me. Now I know what it has been like for you. When I think of my sweet child, all alone after the irises no longer bloom, my heart aches . . ."

"My poor Kae!"

"Mother . . ."

They wept on each other's shoulder. A student nearby who was watching them embrace imagined he was seeing a loving mother and daughter. No hint of a mutual rivalry or feud was apparent. Kae herself felt that their tears were washing away the years of bitterness that had come between them. And, now that her mother-in-law seemed so compassionate, she felt guilty and regretted having hated her for so long. Was Koben's death the penalty she had paid for that hatred? The very possibility brought another stream of tears.

Neither Otsugi nor Kae noticed Koriku observing them with a strange look of disbelief. At thirty-five, Koriku had taken over some of the household chores from her aging mother and assisted Kae as well. Since students were coming to live with the Hanaokas in ever larger numbers, another building had been constructed to house them. But the enormous responsibility of cleaning and supervising meals fell upon Koriku, so that her presence was absolutely indispensable. Yet she was so silent and so rarely asserted herself that no one realized how very valuable she was.

As Otsugi predicted, in about three months Kae began to feel completely drained. Grief was not violently tearing her to pieces as it had done to her mother-in-law. Instead, she wept

more and more often until her eyes burned and severe head-
aches raged in her head. During the day she ignored these
physical ailments, which she believed were due to her solitude
and sorrow, and wiped her eyes and did the housework, often
putting her hand to her forehead. But at night, the mental
and physical anguish was harder to bear. She cried profusely,
the tears running down her face like a flow of thick blood.
Only much later did she discover that a yellowish gummy
substance had been oozing from her eyes.

When Seishu failed to get up for several emergency calls,
Kae surmised that he was taking a sleeping drug, so she
calmly questioned him about it.

"Are you taking some sort of medicine?"

"How did you guess? . . . I've been drinking a mixture that
acts like a powerful sleeping pill. It gets rid of my fatigue."

"That's no joking matter. If anything happens to you while
you're asleep, what could be done, especially since you won't
allow anyone to sleep in your room? Besides, suppose you can't
wake up for a real emergency. Your reputation is at stake."

"Umm. . ." nodded Seishu in frank agreement, though he
was surprised by her tear-filled eyes and unusually accusatory
tone.

"Why don't you give me the medicine?"

"The last preparation I gave you was extremely potent.
After your reactions to it, I realized I had to reduce the dosage.
So you see, Kae, you've done quite enough for me."

"But Mother helped you twice."

"I gave her nothing more than a strong sleeping pill."

Genuinely concerned that Seishu retain the respect and admiration of his numerous patients, Kae at that moment had no
desire to compete with Otsugi. Having lost Koben, her own
life seemed less significant, and the donation of her body to her

husband's research seemed like a worthy action. Whatever her reasoning, she in fact craved the medicine. How she longed to feel the sensation of the blood racing backward through her body! If only she could fall unconscious again. Perhaps a repetition of the previous experiment would alleviate her sorrow. Over and over she implored her husband to give her the drug.

Seishu hesitated for quite a while, hoping to resolve the contradictions within himself. His conscience still bothered him at times because of the large dosage he had already given her. But in the two years of constant research since then he had become more self-confident, and in the end, the desire for a true test of his anesthetic overcame his resistance to experiment once more.

"Well, Kae," he said, holding her hands firmly in his own.

"Yes, my dear." Tears poured forth. Since Koben's death, Kae cried easily. And whenever she did, the pain in her eyes was acute.

Upon hearing of Seishu's intentions, Otsugi knitted her lovely eyebrows together and simply said, "Is that so?" Though her voice was pleasant enough, it lacked the compassion which Kae had been receiving since Koben's funeral.

"Is that so?" repeated Otsugi a second time, obviously displeased. But nothing of a negative nature was expressed in front of Seishu. "Now Kae is in the same frame of mind as I was when I lost Okatsu," she muttered in a barely audible voice as Kae was about to take the drink. Neither Seishu nor his wife understood what she meant.

Seishu held a purple packet containing some dark red powder, and a teacup filled with a small amount of liquor mixed with warm water.

"So little," noted Otsugi.

Kae's anxieties could hardly have been allayed by the sharp, biting tone.

Otsugi, stony-faced and immobile, watched while her son lifted his wife's chin and poured some of his anesthetic, which he called *tsusensan*, into her mouth. She sensed that this final experiment would yield positive results. "How many years of research to make *tsusensan*," she wondered, full of conflicting emotions that prevented her from indulging herself in the joy of her son's imminent success. Sitting poised and elegant considering her sixty-eight years, she thought about her life. All of Seishu's students who had been told the story of her past still considered her unusually beautiful. Nevertheless, she knew that not one of them would deny that she was old. And she was more afraid of aging than of dying.

The *tsusensan* did not produce an immediate effect on Kae. Unlike the former drug, it worked slowly and did not cause chest discomfort. As Kae faded into unconsciousness, she moaned every so often.

"What's the matter?" asked Seishu, bending over her.

Kae faintly shook her head. Otsugi's last words were coming back to her. She understood that she had reached the same frame of mind as her mother-in-law had been in three years ago, when she had first offered to become Seishu's test case. Had Otsugi intended to assert her superiority again? Kae doubted it. In her opinion, Otsugi merely wanted to share her loneliness with another mother who had also lost her daughter. At any rate, Kae was at peace and unafraid. Winning a debate was of no consequence. All she desired was to dream about Koben, but soon she fell under the effect of the drug and became unconscious.

Seishu never left her side although his mother frequently urged him to rest. At midnight, he took Kae's pulse and described her condition in detail. When he rustled her kimono or pinched her thighs, she neither moved nor uttered a sound. And the sashes did not bite into her skin. It was evident from her reactions that the doctor was pleased. Otsugi stared at him continously.

Early the next morning, the subject awoke to a piercing pain in her eyes.

"Kae, are you awake?"

"Yes."

"Can you sit up?"

"Yes, I think so."

Recalling how impossible it had been for her to move the last time, she could now manage to sit with her husband's help. Her fingers trembled as she reached for the cup containing the antidote. In taste, it was very much like the black bean soup of the first experiment, which indicated that the *tsusensan* consisted mainly of *mandarage* and *uzu*. After drinking it, the pain was so unbearable that Kae covered her eyes and fell forward.

"Kae, what's wrong?"

"I'm sorry."

"Tell me how you feel. Tell me everything."

"It's my eyes."

"What?"

"They hurt. I have an awful pain in my head."

His disappointment did not escape Otsugi's notice.

"Kae has cried so much since Koben died that her eyes have become strained. I'm sure her reaction has nothing to do with the medicine. Perhaps some cold water will relieve the ache."

Otsugi left the room, found a towel, and went outside to the well where Koriku and several maids were washing bunches of spring horseradishes.

146

"Mother," called Koriku. "How is Kae?"

"She just got up."

"Really? That was quick."

"I'm sure everything that has happened to her also occurred in the last experiment with me. But she makes such a fuss."

"Why? What is it?"

"She's complaining that her eyes hurt. I suppose a cold compress will help."

"Do you mean for her eyes?" Koriku's face became contorted with fear.

"All those tears since Koben died have weakened them. That's what's the matter. Umpei is worried because he thinks it's been caused by his medicine. Why couldn't she keep quiet? Goodness, she's inconsiderate!"

"Mother!" exclaimed Koriku.

Startled by the loud accusing tone, Otsugi looked up and saw her gentle daughter transformed into an angry woman. The other women were also amazed.

"It's not on account of her tears! And it wasn't after Koben's death that her eyes became weak. Haven't you noticed, Mother? Kae's eyes were affected long before her child got sick. Do you think my patient forebearing sister-in-law would complain for nothing? Mother, you must tell Umpei immediately. If you don't, I will. Kae's eyes hurt because of the medicine she took two years ago."

Otsugi was stupified, as if she had received the lash of a whip. And from her own daughter! As for this new revelation, she had truly not been aware of Kae's problem. Suddenly, while her fingers were in the cold water, she began to shake in an uncontrollable fashion, which prevented her from stopping Koriku, who started for Seishu's room.

"If what Koriku said were true," she reasoned to herself,

"and she isn't the kind to lie—then what about me? Why wasn't I affected by the drug? The experiment only proves how dull and insensitive I really am. An idiot. Now Kae will get all the glory for her sacrifice." She was feeling her age more than ever.

Kae was given a sedative and a cold wet towel over a piece of silk to place on her eyes. Gradually, she stopped groaning.

"Indeed!" Seishu had been questioning his sister about Kae's condition. "I was beginning to deduce that for myself. You see, *tsusensan* should not irritate the eyes. But why wasn't I told sooner about Kae?"

On the one hand, he was obviously happy that the *tsusensan* had behaved as he had anticipated. But on the other, he was resentful and even angry that Kae had never mentioned anything to him. Yet he directed his hostility only toward his mother and sister.

Otsugi was still shivering as she faced his reproaches. "But I . . . I didn't know. Kae never tells me anything."

"Mother!" exclaimed Koriku, and she ran to assist her distressed mother out of the room. Surprised by the thinness of her arms, she gently stroked Otsugi's back, thinking all the while of how old she had become. Not a word was exchanged between them.

Toward noon the pain had definitely subsided enough for Kae to eat a bowl of porridge.

"Sorry you have to worry," she said to her husband.

"Do try to eat," he replied with much tenderness.

Kae sat up by herself and without being prodded began to compare the differences between the two experiments. Overall, she didn't feel too badly, although her head, arms, and legs still felt somewhat numb.

"But . . .," she mumbled shyly, "around here . . ."

148

Through the covers she pointed to the area near her knee. "It hurts, as though I fell."

"I pinched you there. Very hard too. And you didn't budge."

They both laughed.

"Where's Mother?" she inquired after a time.

"She was tired so I told her to rest."

"I'm grateful to her. By the way . . . which midnight is this?" In the bright daylight, Kae blinked several times through watery eyes but could not see her husband.

"Kae. . ." He gently helped her lie down again. "Do they hurt?"

"Not as much."

"Are you sure?"

He lifted her eyelids to examine the pupils. There was no reaction. The thrill of success vanished. From his visibly downcast face, it was clear that the reality of the moment had reached him. The doctor had become a husband. Although Kae could not see it, the black mole on his throat was quivering, indicating that he was trying to fight back tears.

Days passed. The pain diminished and the discharge of mucus ceased altogether. But Kae's sight was completely gone. In constant torment, Seishu's heart was now always with her, even when his mother died like a decayed leaf falling at last to the ground.

When Otsugi was close to death, her blind daughter-in-law could neither take care of her nor see how terribly old she had become. On a night so cold that the herb garden was covered with frost, the woman gasped her last breath. Kae, at that time, was preoccupied with her own nausea as she sat by Otsugi's bed in prayer. And her mother-in-law departed from the world without learning of her pregnancy.

Ryohei, Otsugi's youngest son whom she had urged Seishu to adopt, was still studying medicine in Kyoto. Jihei, the second son, was in Kyoto on business and could not return in time. Only Seishu, Koriku, and Kae were present for the funeral. Otsugi was buried in the Hanaoka graveyard by the Iris Pond.

XIV

In 1801, Kae bore a son whom Seishu called Umpei after his own childhood nickname. When Koriku mentioned that the baby resembled her mother, Kae wasn't the least disturbed, for the deep-seated grudges she had harbored toward her mother-in-law seemed to have disappeared with her death.

"Then Umpei must be a beautiful boy, Koriku," she replied, without a hint of irritation as her sister-in-law continued to care for the baby.

Now that Seishu had his own male child, Kae was less fearful over the matter of Ryohei's adoption, since she knew that her son would succeed her husband even if her brother-in-law were adopted. The long-awaited son! The heir, coveted by both Otsugi and herself. What a thrill it had been to bear him! And after she had given up all hope! For this tiny boy there was ample milk in her breasts, more than required, although she had been unable to nurse Koben. Whenever Koriku brought in the crying baby and placed him on her lap, the eager mother put her nipple to his mouth. It was an act that caused her whole body to feel numb with joy.

Seishu was already a famous doctor, second to none in Kishu province. Around Umpei's second birthday, he appeared as requested before the Kishu lord, who elevated him to the rank of honorary samurai, which permitted him henceforth to wear a sword. Although he treated such worldly honors with indifference, the occasion could not pass without a celebration, particularly since the doctor had some thirty students. Then, as an additional commemoration, Seishu ordered the construction of a separate house for his blind wife and his son, which, though not large, was carefully planned to provide them with the maximum number of conveniences.

Koriku used to drop in with cookies and other delicacies; she adored her nephew and loved to lavish affection on him. But because of her enormous responsibilities and demanding schedule in the Hanaoka household, her visits had to be brief. Seishu, on the other hand, came by often to talk to his wife and play with his son. The house was a relaxing retreat for the busy doctor.

And Kae was happy too. In spite of her present difficulties, the love and kindness of others seemed to provide adequate compensation for the loss of her sight. You might say that her happiness had been purchased in exchange for it. Of course, she was sorry she could not see her child's expressions, or raise him in a normal fashion, but she had no regrets. Her intuition enabled her to sense those visitors that held her in esteem. Besides, when she was out strolling with her maid around Hirayama, she knew that the villagers had stopped their work to look up and nod to one another. Above all, she was aware of the shifting emphasis in the Hanaoka legend—from the story of beautiful Otsugi to the tale of Kae's devotion. What she did not realize was that ever since she had moved into her new house her posture had become erect and graceful, not unlike her deceased mother-in-law's. Whoever happened to drop in found a shapely, poised woman conscious of her physical movements and the fact that she was being observed; she had become similar in so many ways to her former mother-in-law.

"Kae. . ." began Seishu.

"What is it?"

"How would you like to go to a hot spring resort?"

"With your pressing schedule I don't see how we could. Why, you can hardly take the time to relax here."

"I don't mind examining patients. But. . .taking care of the ones who would probably get well anyway . . . it's not enough for me. To tell you the truth, I get bored after I decide who I can cure and who are beyond me. I despise spending day in and day out treating abscesses and all the rest."

While he lay outstretched on the tatami, Kae listened to him from an erect sitting position, both hands placed on her knees. In all of their conversations, she was usually quiet, letting Seishu speak about whatever bothered him. Recalling the years he had been absorbed in research, she knew that unless he was enthusiastic about something, he was sure to become unhappy. And since his work on anesthetics had temporarily come to an end, he was now often irritated and bored, like little Umpei, who would not cheer up until he received a new toy. Nowadays, she understood him very well.

"Kae, my legs . . . you see . . ."

"What's wrong with them?"

"They get stiff. I know it has to do with the experiments I

153

did on myself. But I think it's also a reflection of my impatience with my work."

Kae said nothing. So the poisons had affected her husband too! Now she realized why he either sat with his legs stretched out or lay down when he spoke.

Suddenly shouting came from the main house. Kae was trying to hear what it was all about, and Seishu was lifting himself off the mats when Yonejiro burst in.

"A woman's been gored by a wild bull."

"Where precisely?"

"In her breast . . ." he panted.

Seishu's eyes lit up. "Did you say breast?"

"Yes, her breast. The left one was torn apart, cut open like a pomegranate with the inside exposed. Had it been a man, the horns would have pierced his heart. But I doubt that even a woman will survive this blow."

"How do you know? It's never been proved that a woman can't survive a breast operation. Nobody ever made the test. I'm going right over! Prepare the sutures and disinfectants!"

Kae's heart was pounding as she sensed that the man who raced out of the house like a whirlwind was revitalized. She began to remember past conversations concerning breast surgery: the first night of Seishu's return from Kyoto, and the time he was in agony knowing that he lacked the technique to operate successfully on his sister's cancer. Kae pictured herself sitting next to Okatsu who was close to death, her breasts enlarged, swollen like overripe pumpkins by comparison with her own small ones. Whispering her name, she prayed now to the woman who had been dead over ten years. Perhaps the time had come at last to discover "natural laws by making objective studies" and answer the question: was the breast a vital organ that held the balance of life and death for a woman? Kae tried

154

to visualize her husband—red-eyed and breathing hard as he washed the wound of the woman lying on the huge oilcloth, clotted the blood, applied an anesthetic, and finally sewed her up again. Her prayers lasted for quite a while. She was not praying for the woman's recovery; nor, in fact, did she make any concrete wishes. All she desired was that Seishu discover a new purpose in life so that he might become involved in something as meaningful to him as his work on anesthetics. In those days, completely engrossed in his research, he had never even noticed the feuding that went on between his mother and wife.

Several days passed and Seishu did not come to see his wife. Kae imagined him sitting like a statue beside his patient. In all probability his students were also watching—both their teacher and the woman. Kae inquired about the operation when Koriku came by.

"Well, so far she has survived, so there's a good chance she'll live. That's what they're saying anyway."

"Really?"

"Yes. But if she lives, it means she had a lot of stamina. They told me she's the wife of a peasant and used to very hard work. But look at the pain! My own ears are accustomed to all sorts of noises. Yet I find her groans terrifying! It seems to me that such an operation on an ordinary woman would be fatal. When Okatsu had cancer, I remember that my brother hesitated because he didn't know what to do. In retrospect, I think that even if he had operated on her, she would not have survived the pain."

It was evidently a more aggressive and opinionated Koriku speaking. Either Kae's long periods of silence, or perhaps the heavy household burdens she had assumed after Kae's blindness prompted this outspokenness. In this conversation with

155

Kae she was undoubtedly carried away by the excitement in the main house. Seishu arrived just as his sister finished.

"Kae . . ." he cried in undeniable joy.

"Yes."

"It was superstition as I suspected! It was a myth to connect a woman's breast to her very life. And now I'm waiting for a woman to come, one with breast cancer!"

"I'm happy for you. I've been praying to Okatsu for you since there wasn't anything else I could do."

"Okatsu . . . oh." He frowned and his voice became cross. "I wouldn't be able to save her if she came to me today."

"Why not?"

"There's still the belief that a doctor can't help his own kin."

This conversation preyed on Kae's mind long afterwards, and especially bothered her when Umpei was taking a nap, or on a night when she was completely alone and Seishu did not visit. "Did he consider his wife a blood relation?" she asked herself. Embraced by his gentle warmth in her comfortable home, she never doubted his love. Yet, despite this assurance, it seemed that she, who was once a stranger to the Hanaokas, could never be the true equal of Seishu's parents and siblings. And she strongly believed that her husband felt that way too.

Because of her keen hearing, Kae picked up the symptoms of heavy breathing and raspiness in her sister-in-law's voice. Consequently, she was the first to discover Koriku was seriously ill.

"I know something is wrong, Koriku, and I don't think it's just a question of fatigue. Tell me, what is the trouble?"

"What do you mean?"

"Don't dismiss me that way. It's unfriendly and secretive."

"Speaking of being secretive, are you any better?" She was giggling but her breathing was already rapid.

"Why do you say that?"

"Oh, you want a reason, do you? Well, aren't you having another baby?"

Kae blushed. After moving into the new house, Seishu had grown still more tender and passionate in his lovemaking, so that three years after Umpei's birth, at the age of forty-four, she was indeed pregnant, and of course shy about it, as befitting someone of her age. Koriku noticed that her sister-in-law was unable to find the right words and changed the subject.

"My condition is like Okatsu's in that nothing can be done about it. Feel this lump at the side of my neck. And besides, I'm always tired. At first I thought this sluggishness was due to overweight."

"You said by the side of your neck?"

"Yes." Koriku helped Kae touch the exact spot. It turned out to be in the same place as Seishu's black mole. Fingering it gently, Kae found it as firm as an unripened plum, and with a steady beat like a pulse.

"Maybe it's a hematoma," suggested Koriku, spilling out the word at the same time that Kae thought of it.

There was nothing more to say, and they remained silent. Kae naturally had neither formal medical training nor any specialized knowledge, yet she knew one thing about hematomas, namely, that they were huge swellings in the arteries which drained the person's blood as they grew larger. And like cancer, the malady was still incurable. She had seen many of them in the examination room, all kinds: a hematoma under the arm looking like a ripened persimmon, one at the back of the head which made the person appear to have two heads, and more. What the patients all had in common was the problem of breathing: and when they left the examination room, Kae recalled the despair on their faces.

Once he was informed about his sister, Seishu called her into his room. "I'll have Yonejiro prepare some medicine which you must take faithfully three times a day," he advised her.

"Thank you, Brother."

He was quiet for a long time after her departure to the main house.

"Uh, how is she?" inquired Kae, hesitating to ask.

"Um . . ."

"Is it similar to a hematoma?"

"Yes. But after thinking about it, I've concluded that it's a form of cancer—hemangiosarcoma—a type of cancer in the artery."

"Then it's like Okatsu's case."

"Um . . ."

Signs of life stirred within her; the fetus moved. Kae was struck with the irony of their discussion: speaking of someone doomed to die, while another being was announcing its eventual arrival in the world. It reminded Kae of her morning sickness when Umpei had been in her womb and Otsugi was near death. For the moment it depressed her to think of human beings coming and going.

"Kae . . ." sighed her husband. "Medicine has tremendous depths. Only today I had another patient with breast cancer."

"Really?"

"A strong woman too, eager to have me operate and willing to risk the danger. Anything—as long as I perform the surgery. This will be my first operation for cancer. I've given her something to cure her beriberi before I start. I can't be too careful. But, Kae, I'm confident that my chances are nine out of ten for success. The time has really come . . . that's what I came over to tell you."

"Are you going to use the *tsusensan*?"

"Yes. Can you imagine my restlessness? I simply can't fail. I got so excited thinking about it that I began to shake. I came over to show you how determined I am . . . and to calm my nerves."

"And I told you about Koriku instead. I'm sorry."

"For the moment I felt beaten. You see, even if I cure this breast cancer, as I hope to, I can't say that I will have mastered medicine. I will have only discovered that a woman doesn't die if her breast is opened up. But with hemangiosarcoma, there's no way to operate. Some women commit suicide by stabbing themselves in the throat right on that spot, don't they?"

"So I've been told. You put your hand on your throat, feel for the pulse, and with your mind completely at ease, thrust a dagger into it."

"Koriku's cancer is right there."

Kae didn't know what to say. Nor did Seishu. Finally he snapped in disgust, "I still have a long way to go. No matter how many times the human body is dissected, medicine guards its secrets well."

A few years before Seishu was born, Yamawaki Toyo began dissecting the bodies of dead prisoners. When Seishu reached fifteen, Sugita Genpuku wrote a famous book on anatomy called *Kaitaishinsho*, which was based on Dutch practices as well as on his own experiences. It was an epoch of great achievement for Japanese medicine. But there were no spectacular events or important developments after that. While in Kyoto, Seishu used to tell Asakura Keizan that he was going to find a remedy for the major diseases plaguing the medical world. How spirited and ambitious he had been in those days! Now, he sometimes looked defeated, perhaps because cancer took so many different forms. Even if he succeeded in one operation, he couldn't be too proud: cancer would soon challenge him elsewhere. Up to this point in his life Seishu had been used to many small successes: the ointment he had devised to serve as a local anesthetic during short operations, the countless cases diagnosed accurately and treated, his skillful surgery, and the preparation of new medicines. Yet now that he had the chance to fulfill his lifelong dream, to operate on breast cancer, his prospective joy was clouded with the news of his sister's affliction. Hemangiosarcoma—more dreaded even than breast cancer. Confronted with the reality of his limitations, he could not rejoice at the opportunity he had been waiting for—to prove what he always thought he could do. And Kae's blindness! Although it could be argued that ophthalmology was not his specialty, he was responsible for her. How difficult it was for him to stand by with his arms folded, doing nothing! He bit his lip. There was so much to learn. The fame he would obtain from a successful operation on breast cancer no longer concerned him. His former complacency had given way to a posture of modesty and caution. Before operating on his present patient, he decided to be prudent and allow her plenty of time to recover from her other illnesses. At the same time, he realized that even if he managed to overcome the difficulties of breast cancer, another incurable disease might arise as a by-product of his operation. This was the lesson he had been taught by his wife's blindness.

At the beginning of the following summer, their daughter Kame was born. Koriku was confined to her bed with a hematoma as large as the head of the newborn baby. In fact, it was so hard for her to move that she felt as if she were nailed to it. The lump pressing on her throat prevented her from taking more than warm water and a thin porridge, and she complained of pains in her arms and legs as well. Though Kae was limited in what she could do for her, she had a genuine desire to soothe her suffering sister-in-law. She was more than happy to stay beside her and massage her body. It was a welcome activity for the blind woman.

In one of the small rooms where Kae lived, there were always two beds occupied: one by Koriku and one by the baby. Kae sat between the two, fed the baby when she cried, and rubbed Koriku's body when the pain seemed insupportable.

The weather was oppressive that summer. Kae could tell from her palms that Koriku was getting thinner by the day, hardly eating a morsel and sweating extensively. She wondered which would come first, death from starvation or from the hematoma that was devouring her blood. Once, when she picked her up to help her change her clothing, she was shocked to find that the once-plump woman had become mere skin and bones, like a tree withering away. She wept quietly.

"Are you crying, Sister?" asked Koriku in a thin, rasping voice. Close to death, she was still perfectly lucid.

"It's funny that the tears come even though I can't see," replied Kae, trying to make a joke.

"Why are you crying?"

"You call me 'Sister.' But I haven't done anything for you. Forgive me."

"What nonsense. I haven't anything against you."

"On account of me you didn't get married. Instead of having a home of your own, you took over all of my responsibilities. Now you're sick . . . in this house . . . I want you to get completely well again."

"Sister, if you mean that"—each word was distinct— "if you mean marriage, not only have I not regretted it, but as I lie here near death, I feel most fortunate. You know I watched

161

everything that happened between you and my mother. What a horrible relationship that was! My younger sisters came home several months ago to attend a memorial service for my mother; and all they could say were nasty things about their mothers-in-law. They talked, and I just listened. I hoped they would feel better if they got their misery off their chest. Conflicts between women don't exist in this house alone, you see. They are everywhere. Every family winds up struggling with the same problems as the generation before. Why does a woman bother to dress up for her wedding in a gorgeous bridal kimono? By the next morning, it will all vanish in smoke anyway. Okatsu and I will die from similar diseases. But in spite of our terrible suffering, I think it will have been easier for us this way than going through what you did."

"Koriku, how can you talk like that? It's absurd. Your deceased mother requested my presence here. Your beautiful, intelligent mother treated me like her own daughter!"

"Oh, you don't have to pretend in front of me. I couldn't take either side because she was my own mother. But nothing escaped me."

"Don't say that, Koriku. Besides, all this chatter will tire you out. You must rest now."

"Sister . . . " persisted Koriku, ignoring Kae's wishes and adopting a more spiteful manner. "Why don't you regret taking medicine that made you blind? You knew very well it was dangerous. But you drank it anyway, just to compete with Mother. Why? My brother became famous and people think you and Mother are wonderful."

"What in the world are you trying to say, Koriku?" Kae was abashed. Koriku's observations had shaken her and she couldn't find a suitable reply to all those accusations. But she felt she ought to let them pass, maintain their conversation, and try to divert Koriku from her present subject. "Mother was an admirable woman. I really believe that. Thanks to her I led a useful life as a doctor's wife. Of course, I often displeased her. After all, I wasn't her own daughter, and I was stubborn besides. But from the bottom of my heart, I think she was splendid. 'Vanish in smoke?' Really, that's ridiculous."

"Do you actually feel that way?"

"Indeed I do," nodded Kae to convince Koriku that she was doubly certain. And since she truly seemed to believe her own words, she didn't bear the guilty burden of lying.

In Koriku's scrawny face, only her eyes bulged, much like Seishu's. Kae, of course, couldn't see them, and was sitting rather quiescently with her own eyes closed when Koriku snapped back:

"If you feel that way, it's because you won!"

Kae felt as if lightning had just struck her, and she neither drew breath nor moved. Her blindness had not protected her from Koriku's attack, and she was unable to deny the cool, relentless, penetrating judgments of her dying sister-in-law. Still, she refused to panic.

The silence between them lasted for some time. Koriku also closed her eyes and tried to control her breathing. After a while, with her eyes still shut, she spoke again. Her voice was hoarse, for she was clearly in pain, as she rambled on and intermittently paused for breath.

"Don't you think men are incredible? It seems . . . that an intelligent person like my brother . . . would have noticed the friction between you and Mother. . . . But throughout he shrewdly pretended he didn't see anything . . . which resulted in both you and Mother drinking the medicine. . . . Well, isn't it so? . . . I think this sort of tension among females . . . is . . . to the advantage . . . of . . . every male. And I doubt

163

that any man would volunteer to mediate in their struggles."
She tried to clear her throat. "He would probably be considered weak if he did, and I suspect . . . he would perish like
an over-fertilized mandarin tree."

Then, after a long pause, "Come to think of it, Sister, isn't
the relationship between man and woman disgusting? Of
course, I'm excluding brothers and sisters. Suppose you had
gotten my disease. Seishu might have taken a knife and operated. But he wouldn't do it to his sister. Maybe that's why sisters
are expected to get married. . . . They're of no use to their
brothers. I'm sure this has been true for past generations and
will continue to be so forever . . . as long as there are men and
women side by side on this earth. I wouldn't want to be reborn
as a woman into such a world. The only luck I've had in my
entire lifetime is that I didn't get married and didn't have to be
somebody's daughter-in-law or mother-in-law."

Kae was beyond trying to stop her. And if she had tried, Koriku would have kept on anyway. It seemed that once Koriku
stopped talking, she would have no energy left to maintain
her small, weightless form. Pretty soon, Kae felt as if her brain
had been wrenched open, and she began to sense the truth of
Koriku's judgments.

Seishu rarely came to visit his dying sister. Perhaps, since he
had no hope of curing her, it was too painful for him to watch
his own flesh and blood fade away. But a more realistic reason
may have been that he was too preoccupied with the patient
he intended to operate on, with reviewing previous medical
data and records of his other patients on whom he had conduct-
ed surgery. He may even have been rereading *Honzo Komoku*
from the beginning again. Kae could visualize him even
better now than before she had become blind.

The patient with the breast cancer whom Seishu had been

telling Kae about was the mother of Rihei, owner of a dye works in Yamato. Her name was Kan and she was sixty years old. Some time before she discovered a hard lump in her breast which was correctly diagnosed by her local doctor as cancer. However, he did not give her any medicine and simply admitted that there was no cure for her. Due to the nature of his business, Rihei was quick to hear of news from all over Japan, and consequently learned of a famous doctor in Kishu who spectacularly cured all sorts of strange diseases. Thus, he brought his mother all the way from the neighboring region to see him. The old woman was anxious for an operation, partly because she had already given up hope of recovering and wanted to go before the cancer became fully developed, and partly because she preferred to die by the hand of a well-known doctor. She begged Seishu to operate with a unique, peculiar enthusiasm, while he was still in the midst of pondering the proper procedure.

On October 13, 1805, the same year that Kame was born, Seishu completed the preliminaries and administered *tsusensan* to Kan, who was lying on an oilcloth in the operating room. After he was sure that the drug was acting properly, the confident Seishu put on his persimmon-colored linen surgical coat with the help of an assistant. It was decorated with five loops sewn on like family crests on a formal kimono—one on the back and two others on the front and back of each sleeve; the entire design had been created by the doctor himself. When he put a string through the loops and pulled, his sleeves were automatically raised, giving his arms freedom of movement. The loop was shaped exactly as the tie Kae had bound her legs with during the experiments; it was later printed as a crest on his formal wear, for the doctor wore the invention with pride to show that he had not forgotten his wife's collaboration in his

165

work. The original paulownia family crest was handed down to his brother Ryohei. As for the details of the operation, they were recorded by Seishu in his *Records on Cures for Breast Cancer*. Here is the excerpt.

Winter morning of October 13: I gave the patient a dose of *mafutsusan*. Soon she began to fade into a coma and completely lost consciousness. Her whole body was numb under the anesthetic. Using a *koromushitsusu* knife, as shown in Figure 2, I cut vertically three inches above the tumor. The bleeding was profuse. I clotted the blood. Then I inserted the fingers of both hands and exerted much effort in order to isolate the tumor from the surrounding flesh. I found sinews which I cut through with a *koromushitsusu* knife just as I would cut a nerve. More bleeding ensued and was easily controlled. Gradually, the flesh became loose and the tumor was removed. Afterwards, I washed the wound with alcohol and put some *harusamkoppaiha* into it to stop the bleeding. I sewed it with thread, applied ointment as one would to an ordinary sword wound. I added some salt to warm rice broth and had the patient drink it as an antidote to the *mafutsusan*, and then gave her licorice and thin porridge for nourishment. When she finally came to her senses, she looked up at the wound on her breast in surprise. "Where's the lump? The swelling is gone. How wonderul! I didn't even know it had happened. There was no pain. Why, the swelling and tumor have disappeared!"

At the beginning of the same record Seishu had written: "I'm going to cure breast cancer by modelling my technique after Hua Tu's." The line explains why Seishu called the anesthetic *mafutsusan*—that is, after Hua Tu's experiments with narcotic water—and not *tsusensan*. But although he claimed to have imitated Hua Tu, there were no records of the venerable medical genius of some seventeen centuries earlier, so Seishu must be fully credited for the first operation. The allusion to Hua Tu here may have furthermore been prompted by the vivid memories the doctor retained of his childhood hero, and emphasizes at the same time the extent of his enthusiasm for performing the above operation.

It was not only a great personal victory for Seishu. The operation was in fact the first in world history to be performed under general anesthesia. Dr. Long in the United States operated with ether in 1842, and Dr. Simpson, a British gynecologist, used chloroform in 1847. But both of these cases came respectively thirty-seven and forty-two years after Hanaoka Seishu's. It can be said that the achievement of the Japanese doctor was responsible for the greatest leap in the development of surgery, which until that time had been an old-fashioned, stagnant field. Aside from this, it opened the new domain of so-called difficult operations.

Seishu's sister had her throat choked by the hematoma and died quietly, without a voice, one month before his glorious triumph. She was forty-two and remained lucid until the end. A tombstone was erected for her in the Hanaoka cemetery. She could not have guessed that one hundred and fifty years later, her brother's great accomplishment would be noted at the International Conference on Surgery, or that a picture in the Japanese tradition depicting the devoted Otsugi and Kae in the experiment would be hung in Chicago's Hall of Fame, together with other articles belonging to the famous doctor.

In the midst of the excitement over Seishu, only Kae, with tears streaming down her cheeks, burned incense and prayed for Koriku at the altar. She imagined that the souls of Otsugi and Koriku could repose in peace now that Seishu's ambition was fulfilled. Still, the bitterness of Koriku's remark, "It's because you won," stuck in her mind.

Toward the end of the month, Seishu finally visited his wife.

"You must have heard about my marvelous success, Kae. It was all accomplished thanks to you and Mother. Soon, every single doctor all over Japan will be astonished by it."

He was brimming with happiness. Although he tried to control himself and not boast in front of his students, he had no such inhibitions before his wife. Kae was also overjoyed, at least outwardly. In her heart, however, she felt ashamed. She really did not believe that she had been useful to him or that she had contributed to his success as he had just said.

"Congratulations. How happy Mother would be!" She was self-conscious, and with every word felt as if she were being criticized by her dead sister-in-law.

XV

The number of students studying under the doctor rose steadily until the enrollment reached well over one hundred. His surgical procedure for cancer using general anesthesia was such a great success that it brought distinction to his small village. From Tsugaru in the north to Satsuma in the south they came to Nate in Kishu province, and it was rapidly becoming a gathering place for members of the medical profession. The Hanaoka facilities were hopelessly inadequate to accommodate all the newcomers seeking to study there, no matter how many wings were added, so Seishu eventually purchased some local land on which a new, larger building was constructed. The central area, consisting of examination and operating rooms, was connected by a corridor to the family quarters. A section for the seriously ill was located in another area that also contained rooms for students and assistants, as well as a storage depository for medicines and a pharmacy. In addition, there were servants' quarters, a stable for two horses, a large repository for valuable items, and a storehouse for rice and other supplies. In all, the collection of buildings encompassed over six hundred and fifty square meters, ten times the size of the original house with its tiny herb garden of *mandarage*. When the great structure was finally crowned with a tile roof, the entire building shone. Indeed it was an object of beauty for all Hirayama to behold. Seishu called it "Shunrinken," literally meaning "The House of the Spring Forest," because of its fresh wood aroma, and had the name inscribed on a tablet and hung at the entrance. Among the students, it was referred to as the "Shunrinken House of Study." Scores of young men vied for the chance to serve as interns there.

Students of surgery were not its only inhabitants. The sick, accompanied by their families, came there from everywhere, though of course Shunrinken could not possibly lodge them all. Several new inns, such as the Kaikaido with its adjacent restaurant, had to be constructed in Hirayama and became very popular due to their affiliation with the doctor. Later on, still another inn called Hoteiya was built, and provided housing for those students who could not find accommodation at Shunrinken itself. Soon, many farmers began to accept boarders. Little by little the isolated village of Hirayama bustled with increasing activity.

Tokugawa Harutomi, the tenth lord of Kishu, committed himself to bringing culture to his region. Toward this end, he invited prominent scholars, for example, Motoori Norinaga from Ise, to help advance his new educational programs and promote the study of Neo-Confucianism. Advised by the chief of the medical bureau, he also established a state school. It was unlikely, therefore, that Lord Harutomi would overlook Hanaoka Seishu, whose fame had spread throughout Japan.

By 1802, he had already promoted Seishu to the rank of honorary samurai, though at that time, the doctor had most respectfully declined an offer to become the lord's personal physician. Seishu explained that public office would greatly hamper his first duty, which was to heal ordinary people. A precedent for such a refusal had been set by Hua Tu, who according to legend turned down a similar request by Ts'ao Ts'ao of the Wei dynasty. It became a point of honor, however, for the lord to employ Seishu in an official capacity, and he persisted until the doctor finally acceded, and in 1813, accepted the post of associate physician. But he was granted permission to maintain his residence in Hirayama. In 1819 he was elevated to the position of state physician, and in 1833 to surgeon general and chief physician for Kishu province. The honorable post required by custom that the doctor shave his head, but Seishu preferred to keep his locks long like Chinese doctors. And he had his way. He was allowed such unprecedented freedom in part because of his personality, but more so because of his influence in the medical world.

As the Hanaoka method and treatment achieved recognition, Seishu received scores of letters, including one from Sugita Genpaku, the famous pioneer and scholar in Western medicine. The modest fashion in which he asked for instruction will give the reader some idea of Seishu's reputation.

May 4

Dear Dr. Hanaoka:

I have not yet had the honor of making your acquaintance, but please permit me to write to you. The days are getting warmer and I am happy to hear that you are in good health and doing well. Your name is well known as far as Edo. Miyakawa Juntatsu, a student from Kaga who spent last year studying with you, came up to Edo and told me about you and how hard you've been working at your practice and research. While I serve as the personal physican of the lord here, I would like to make myself available to cure the illnesses from which common people suffer. Yet the days pass, and I regret that I haven't made my contribution. I am now eighty years old. But old as I am, I intend to be of some use whenever the opportunity arises. I frequently have questions that cannot be answered by anyone in my field, so I find it most fortunate to have found someone like yourself in the medical profession. Juntatsu has described your amazing skill in performing operations. I am truly impressed.

Do you get news from Edo? Very often there are people who need surgery here, but there is no one in this area who is brave enough to assume the responsibility. I would like to help, and, as I said, regret very much that I am helpless and must pass up such cases. Hereafter, I would like to consult with you by mail, and hope you can answer my questions. As I'm getting old, I ask you to please extend this favor to my sons whenever they seek your advice.

Once again, forgive the liberty I have taken in writing to you. I did so at Juntatsu's insistence, and beg that I may be included among your acquaintances.

Respectfully yours,
Sugita Genpaku

According to the contents of the letter, Sugita Genpaku was eighty years old. Hanaoka Seishu was then fifty-three. The courtesy and respect with which the famous scholar addressed the younger country doctor clearly indicates Sugita's noble character. As for the letter itself, Seishu was so appreciative that he retained it as a family treasure.

Out of the old story of Otsugi and Naomichi, a new legend was born about the prosperous Hanaokas. At its core was the theme of devotion attributed to the mother and the wife of Seishu, and how they built the foundation for the present-day grandeur of Shunrinken. Shimomura Ryoan and Imose Yonejiro, who were now the managers of the family school, frequently told it. Seishu himself was never reluctant to emphasize the tremendous support he had received from his mother and Kae. To his wife, whom he sincerely loved, he showed his devotion in many ways, sometimes by inviting *Joruri* players to Shunrinken to perform their ballads. Kae remained a rather shy, unobtrusive person, becoming even more retiring and quiet as the years passed, living in peace and away from crowds. It was also apparent that she did not like hearing the story at all. People thought it was due to her modesty. But despite her feelings, her blindness and dignity only magnified the drama of the tale, and it eventually became a legend.

She died in 1829 at the age of sixty-eight, her eyes and lips sealed forever. Villagers and students alike attended the elaborate funeral. In fact, anyone who had any connection whatsoever with Shunrinken came to mourn for this incomparably wise woman. When she was laid to rest in the Hanaoka cemetery by the Iris Pond, her tombstone appeared one size larger than the one behind her which belonged to Otsugi—a difference due perhaps to the increased prosperity of the family. Her stone, which overshadowed Otsugi's, was inscribed simply with her posthumous Buddhist name.

Even larger than twice the size of the two women's tombs combined is that of Seishu, who died six years after his wife.

It stands on a triple pedestal six feet high, towering over all the others in the Hanaoka cemetery. On the front of the blue stone is his posthumous Buddhist name, and on the west side, "Died October 2, sixth year of Tenpo (1835), at the age of seventy-six."

If you stand directly in front of Seishu's tomb, the two behind him, those of Kae and Otsugi, are completely obscured.

（新装版）英文版 華岡青洲の妻
The Doctor's Wife

2003年11月14日　第1刷発行

著　者　　有吉佐和子

訳　者　　広中和歌子、アン・コスタント

発行者　　畑野文夫

発行所　　講談社インターナショナル株式会社
　　　　　〒112-8652　東京都文京区音羽 1-17-14
　　　　　電話　03-3944-6493（編集部）
　　　　　　　　03-3944-6492（営業部・業務部）
　　　　　ホームページ　www.kodansha-intl.co.jp

印刷・製本所　　大日本印刷株式会社

JAPANESE LANGUAGE GUIDES

Easy-to-use guides to essential language skills

13 SECRETS FOR SPEAKING FLUENT JAPANESE
日本語をペラペラ話すための13の秘訣　*Giles Murray*

The most fun, rewarding, and universal techniques of successful learners of Japanese that anyone can put immediately to use. A unique and exciting alternative, full of lively commentaries, comical illustrations, and brain-teasing puzzles.

Paperback, 184 pages; ISBN 4-7700-2302-2

ALL ABOUT PARTICLES　新装版 助詞で変わるあなたの日本語　*Naoko Chino*

The most common and less common particles brought together and broken down into some 200 usages, with abundant sample sentences.

Paperback, 160 pages; ISBN 4-7700-2781-8

JAPANESE VERBS AT A GLANCE　新装版 日本語の動詞　*Naoko Chino*

Clear and straightforward explanations of Japanese verbs—their functions, forms, roles, and politeness levels.

Paperback, 180 pages; ISBN 4-7700-2765-6

BEYOND POLITE JAPANESE: A Dictionary of Japanese Slang and Colloquialisms
新装版 役に立つ話しことば辞典　*Akihiko Yonekawa*

Expressions that all Japanese, but few foreigners, know and use every day. Sample sentences for every entry.

Paperback, 176 pages; ISBN 4-7700-2773-7

BUILDING WORD POWER IN JAPANESE: Using Kanji Prefixes and Suffixes
新装版 増えて使えるヴォキャブラリー　*Timothy J. Vance*

Expand vocabulary and improve reading comprehension by modifying your existing lexicon.

Paperback, 128 pages; ISBN 4-7700-2799-0

HOW TO SOUND INTELLIGENT IN JAPANESE: A Vocabulary Builder
新装版 日本語の知的表現　*Charles De Wolf*

Lists, defines, and gives examples for the vocabulary necessary to engage in intelligent conversation in fields such as politics, art, literature, business, and science.

Paperback, 160 pages; ISBN 4-7700-2859-8

MAKING SENSE OF JAPANESE: What the Textbooks Don't Tell You
新装版 日本語の秘訣　*Jay Rubin*

"Brief, wittily written essays that gamely attempt to explain some of the more frustrating hurdles [of Japanese].... They can be read and enjoyed by students at any level."　—*Asahi Evening News*

Paperback, 144 pages; ISBN 4-7700-2802-4

LOVE, HATE and Everything in Between: Expressing Emotions in Japanese
新装版 日本語の感情表現集　*Mamiko Murakami*

Includes more than 400 phrases that are useful when talking about personal experience and nuances of feeling.

Paperback, 176 pages; ISBN 4-7700-2803-2

JAPANESE LANGUAGE GUIDES

Easy-to-use guides to essential language skills

THE HANDBOOK OF JAPANESE VERBS

日本語動詞ハンドブック　*Taeko Kamiya*

An indispensable reference and guide to Japanese verbs aimed at beginning and intermediate students. Precisely the book that verb-challenged students have been looking for.

• Verbs are grouped, conjugated, and combined with auxiliaries　• Different forms are used in sentences
• Each form is followed by reinforcing examples and exercises

Paperback, 256 pages; ISBN 4-7700-2683-8

THE HANDBOOK OF JAPANESE ADJECTIVES AND ADVERBS

日本語形容詞・副詞ハンドブック　*Taeko Kamiya*

The ultimate reference manual for those seeking a deeper understanding of Japanese adjectives and adverbs and how they are used in sentences. Ideal, too, for those simply wishing to expand their vocabulary or speak livelier Japanese.

Paperback , 336 pages; ISBN 4-7700-2879-2

A HANDBOOK OF COMMON JAPANESE PHRASES

日本語決まり文句辞典　*Sanseido*

Japanese is rich in common phrases perfect for any number and variety of occasions. This handbook lists some 600 of them and explains when, where, and how to use them, providing alternatives for slightly varied circumstances and revealing their underlying psychology.

Paperback, 320 pages; ISBN 4-7700-2798-2

BASIC CONNECTIONS: Making Your Japanese Flow

新装版 日本語の基礎ルール　*Kakuko Shoji*

Explains how words and phrases dovetail, how clauses pair up with other clauses, how sentences come together to create harmonious paragraphs. The goal is to enable the student to speak both coherently and smoothly.

Paperback, 160 pages; ISBN 4-7700-2860-1

JAPANESE CORE WORDS AND PHRASES: Things You Can't Find in a Dictionary

新装版 辞書では解らない慣用表現　*Kakuko Shoji*

Some Japanese words and phrases, even though they lie at the core of the language, forever elude the student's grasp. This book brings these recalcitrants to bay.

Paperback, 144 pages; ISBN 4-7700-2774-5

READ REAL JAPANESE: All You Need to Enjoy Eight Contemporary Writers

新装版 日本語で読もう　*Janet Ashby*

Original Japanese essays by Yoko Mori, Ryuichi Sakamoto, Machi Tawara, Shoichi Nejime, Momoko Sakura, Seiko Ito, Banana Yoshimoto, and Haruki Murakami. With vocabulary lists giving the English for Japanese words and phrases and also notes on grammar, nuance, and idiomatic usage.

Paperback, 168 pages; ISBN 4-7700-2936-5

BREAKING INTO JAPANESE LITERATURE: Seven Modern Classics in Parallel Text

日本語を読むための七つの物語　*Giles Murray*

Read classics of modern Japanese fiction in the original with the aid of a built-in, customized dictionary, free MP3 sound files of professional Japanese narrators reading the stories, and literal English translations. Features Ryunosuke Akutagawa's "Rashomon" and other stories.

Paperback, 240 pages; ISBN 4-7700-2899-7

KODANSHA INTERNATIONAL DICTIONARIES

Easy-to-use dictionaries designed for non-native learners of Japanese.

KODANSHA'S FURIGANA JAPANESE DICTIONARY
JAPANESE-ENGLISH / ENGLISH-JAPANESE　ふりがな和英・英和辞典

Both of Kodansha's popular furigana dictionaries in one portable, affordable volume. A truly comprehensive and practical dictionary for English-speaking learners, and an invaluable guide to using the Japanese language.
• 30,000-word basic vocabulary　• Hundreds of special words, names, and phrases
• Clear explanations of semantic and usage differences　• Special information on grammar and usage
Hardcover, 1318 pages; ISBN 4-7700-2480-0

KODANSHA'S FURIGANA JAPANESE-ENGLISH DICTIONARY
新装版 ふりがな和英辞典

The essential dictionary for all students of Japanese.
• Furigana readings added to all *kanji*　• 16,000-word basic vocabulary
Paperback, 592 pages; ISBN 4-7700-2750-8

KODANSHA'S FURIGANA ENGLISH-JAPANESE DICTIONARY
新装版 ふりがな英和辞典

The companion to the essential dictionary for all students of Japanese.
• Furigana readings added to all *kanji*　• 14,000-word basic vocabulary
Paperback, 728 pages; ISBN 4-7700-2751-6

KODANSHA'S ROMANIZED JAPANESE-ENGLISH DICTIONARY
新装版 ローマ字和英辞典

A portable reference written for beginning and intermediate students.
• 16,000-word basic vocabulary　• No knowledge of *kanji* necessary
Paperback, 688 pages; ISBN 4-7700-2753-2

KODANSHA'S CONCISE ROMANIZED JAPANESE-ENGLISH DICTIONARY
コンサイス版 ローマ字和英辞典

A first, basic dictionary for beginner students of Japanese.
• 10,000-word basic vocabulary　• Easy-to-find romanized entries listed in alphabetical order
• Definitions written for English-speaking users
• Sample sentences in romanized and standard Japanese script, followed by English translations
Paperback, 480 pages; ISBN 4-7700-2849-0

KODANSHA'S BASIC ENGLISH-JAPANESE DICTIONARY
日本語学習 基礎英日辞典

An annotated dictionary useful for both students and teachers.
• Over 4,500 headwords and 18,000 vocabulary items　• Examples and information on stylistic differences
• Appendices for technical terms, syntax and grammar
Paperback , 1520 pages; ISBN 4-7700-2895-4

THE MODERN ENGLISH-NIHONGO DICTIONARY
日本語学習 英日辞典

The first truly bilingual dictionary designed exclusively for non-native learners of Japanese.
• Over 6,000 headwords　• Both standard Japanese (with *furigana*) and romanized orthography
• Sample sentences provided for most entries　• Numerous explanatory notes and *kanji* guides
Vinyl flexibinding, 1200 pages; ISBN 4-7700-2148-8

JAPANESE SPIRITUALITY AND CULTURE

HAGAKURE The Book of the Samurai　*Yamamoto Tsunetomo*　葉隠　山本常朝 著

Hagakure ("In the Shadow of Leaves") is a manual for the samurai classes consisting of a series of short anecdotes and reflections that give both insight and instruction in the philosophy and code of behavior that foster the true spirit of Bushido—the Way of the Warrior. As featured in the film *Ghost Dog.*
Hardcover, 192 pages; ISBN 4-7700-2916-0　Paperback, 184 pages; ISBN 4-7700-1106-7

THE BOOK OF FIVE RINGS　*Miyamoto Musashi*　五輪書　宮本武蔵 著

Setting down his thoughts on swordplay, on winning, and on spirituality, legendary swordsman Miyamoto Musashi intended this modest work as a guide for his immediate disciples and future generations of samurai. He had little idea he was penning a masterpiece that would be eagerly devoured by people in all walks of life centuries after his death.
Hardcover, 160 pages; ISBN 4-7700-2801-6

MUSASHI An Epic Novel of the Samurai Era　*Eiji Yoshikawa*　宮本武蔵　吉川英治 著

This classic work tells of the legendary samurai who was the greatest swordsman of all time.
"… a stirring saga … one that will prove popular not only for readers interested in Japan but also for those who simply want a rousing read."　　　　　　—*The Washington Post*
Hardcover, 984 pages; ISBN 4-7700-1957-2

BUSHIDO The Soul of Japan　*Inazo Nitobe*　武士道　新渡戸稲造 著

Written specifically for a Western audience in 1900 by Japan's under-secretary general to the League of Nations, *Bushido* explains concepts such as honor and loyalty within traditional Japanese ethics. The book is a classic, and as such throws a great deal of light on Japanese thinking and behavior, both past and present.
Hardcover , 160 pages; ISBN 4-7700-2731-1

THE UNFETTERED MIND　Writings of the Zen Master to the Sword Master

Soho Takuan　不動智神妙録　沢庵宗彭 著

The philosophy and competitive strategy presented by the spiritual mentor to Musashi is as useful to today's corporate warriors as it was to 17th-century samurai.
Hardcover , 144 pages; ISBN 4-7700-2947-0　Paperback, 104 pages; ISBN 0-87011-851-X

THE BOOK OF TEA　*Kakuzo Okakura*　茶の本　岡倉覚三 著

The seminal text on the meaning and practice of tea. Written 80 years ago, the book is less about tea than it is about the philosophical and aesthetic traditions basic to Japanese culture.
Paperback, 168 pages; ISBN 4-7700-1542-9

THE ANATOMY OF DEPENDENCE　*Takeo Doi, M.D.*　甘えの構造　土居健郎 著

The classic analysis of *amae,* the indulging, passive love which supports an individual within a group, and a key concept in Japanese psychology.
"Profound insights not only into the character of Japan but into the nuances of dependency relationships." —*Ezra Vogel*　　　　　　Paperback, 192 pages; ISBN 4-7700-2800-8

THE ANATOMY OF SELF The Individual Versus Society　*Takeo Doi, M.D.*

表と裏　土居健郎 著

A fascinating exploration of the role of the individual in Japan, and Japanese concepts of self-awareness, communication, and relationships.　Paperback, 176 pages; ISBN 4-7700-2779-6

WORDS IN CONTEXT　*Takao Suzuki*　ことばと文化　鈴木孝夫 著

One of Japan's foremost linguists offers a provocative analysis of the complex relationship between language and culture, psychology and lifestyle.
Paperback, 192 pages; ISBN 4-7700-2780-X

JAPANESE LITERATURE

ANTHOLOGIES

HAIKU

The 20th Anniversary
Presentation
By HIFA
Hashimoto-city
International Friendship Association